W

REA

THE WRANGLESNITCH ROBBERY

A robbery in town

WANTED

READ OR ALIVE:
THE WRANGLESNITCH ROBBERY

A SERIES OF ALIBIS
BY THE YEAR 4 STUDENTS OF
NEWTON FARM NURSERY,
INFANT & JUNIOR SCHOOL

CONTENTS

The Prologue
A Letter From Dean Yapperspoke

You could probably tell it was already Autumn by the chill dancing under the dying sun. An early sunset by any design is a good signal that your usual troublemakers are bound to be at large sooner rather than later. Up in the gigantic, mountainous fjords of Wranglesnitch Town, the final day of the summer finally met its demise, and the sun sank into her hiding place behind the mountain peaks. A breeding ground for trouble—as you always liked to describe it, back during our prime years together on the force.

You and I both know, Detective, that Wranglesnitch isn't a place known for unexpected trouble – or anything "*out of the ordinary*" at all, for that matter. It's pretty sound – at least, prior to the sun going down. As for the town's small population, their haven in the mountains was always the perfect escape from the watchful, and sometimes critical, eyes of the outside world. The loyal and trusting folks of Wranglesnitch are satisfied with their isolated environment and they're happy to keep it that way. Loneliness is their only concept of homeliness.

From what I'm being told so far, the events went roughly something like this: It was a Sunday evening, an early end to a tired weekend wander for many—window-shopping, hop-scotching, gossiping, and whatnot—and so there remained little room in their calm spirits for overexerting any kind of concern. As was the norm at this time, the town closed their weekend businesses and then retired to their homes to spend the rest of the day with their nearest and dearest, families and friends alike.

Down in the town's cute, little market square of cobbled pavements and narrowly winding roads, the owners of the local bakery switched off its final oven a little after 4PM, for Sunday Dinner rarely demanded a side of baguettes or a starchy chocolate cake for dessert. Just outside of the quaint market square stood the deserted Pigeonhole Postal Tower, where flocks of delivery birds from across the mountain range commonly come to collect the town's letters from the tower's gaping open crevices and carried them to the furthest unknown lands of the outside world. On the corner of the street, the fire station turned over its final shift and the last of the working firefighters went home, almost arrogantly knowing there were forever going to be no calls for any fires on that cold, leafy evening. And even as high as the luxurious towers of *The Harrowing-Leigh High Hotel*, the lights of the hotel restaurant and lobby dimmed for the evening retreat, so as not to disturb its very picky and easily displeased guests.

Meanwhile, somehow, Anderson's Dockyard Fishery remained open oddly later than usual, since – according to the head fisherman, Mr. Anderson – they had been behind on their catch for most of the day. Overall, everything remained peacefully untouched for the remainder of the afternoon and peace prevailed long into the night. That was until the moonlight let itself in through the town's backdoor, and an unfamiliar shadow crept through the silent streets of Wranglesnitch...

It may have been a peaceful night for many in Wranglesnitch that night. Such serene silence, however, worked to one sinister individual's advantage. We predict that, at approximately fifteen minutes past the hour of midnight, this very individual burdened the town with the greatest pain it had ever experienced in its history. The hidden silhouette emerged from the trees of the surrounding forest, tiptoed over the cobbles of the market square, edging unnoticeably towards where Mr. Anderson's dockyard sat at the end of the town's pier. The suspect then stole a boat from the pier and discreetly sailed it across the small lake, towards the Pigeonhole Postal Tower that sat isolated on one of the waterlogged islands.

Once they had reached the island, the shadowy figure wasted no time entering the building and scaled the curling staircase all the way to the very top of the tower, where there was laid a sack of letters belonging to the humble townspeople. These special, private letters were full of hidden emotion and suppressed beliefs – secret words they had written to be shared with nobody, except their trusting recipients far away from Wranglesnitch. Our suspect snatched the sack in its entirety and disappeared into obscurity again, this time with all of the town's mail in his possession and escaping upstream in his stolen boat – leaving not one single letter behind.

By morning light, everybody's mail was gone.

As the sun began to peek over the horizon on the following Monday morning, and the first weary heads began to rise and emerge from their bungalows, the horrifying reality that had become of their usually safe and undisturbed haven dawned upon them as quickly as the growing daylight. I had the task of consoling those who had lost their valuable letters from the Postal Tower. Each and every one of them felt as though something very close to their heart had been robbed from them. Several suspects were arrested at the scene, those who had access to the dockyard near to the time that the robbery was committed – including Mister Bartholomew Anderson, the town's head fisherman, who sits in a cell today, voicing his apparent innocence from bottom of his breathless, worn-out lungs.

'Why do you think it is, Mister Anderson, that you of all people were plucked out as a prime suspect in the investigation of this robbery?' I asked the aforementioned suspect.

Mr. Anderson shrugged heavily, exhausted from pleading the same words of his innocence and injustice over and over again.

'Out on the docks, long after everybody else had returned home, you were still claiming to be fishing there,' I elaborated. 'It seems a bit unusual, doesn't it.'

'You're asking the wrong sailor the right questions, Mister Yapperspoke,' the old fisherman spat back at me. He seemed to be offended by the fact that I was having to ask him any questions at all, more so than what I was *actually asking* him.

'Well, if you're so sure you're clean, then who do you propose that I interrogate instead?' I persisted badgering him for some measly inch of an answer.

'Me don't have any interest for reading too deeply into people's personal lives. This town is built on the principle of trust. It really is as simple as that. Find out whoever is the least trustworthy in this town and you'll catch your culprit,' the fisherman added finally. 'If you're trying to uncover who is responsible for stealing those letters, I'd start with asking those who are keeping their head low. You know who I mean, the folks in that town who have nothing to say – *apparently*.'

Maybe the stubborn old barnacle was right – there was too much quiet in town in the wake of such an atrocity. Someone was using the silence as shield. After ending that interrogation with the veteran fisherman, I'm still a bit stuck for answers to this mess, partner. I need your help, or any more support you can find. You may need to do some investigating on the side and report back with some suspects of your own. Can I ask that you join me for this one last case, partner? *Pretty please!*

This is my confidential account of the affair. Share this information with no one, unless they are strictly involved with the case. Please message me if you have any further queries about the crime or my suspects. I look forward to seeing what you have to contribute. Until you do, God help the folk of Wranglesnitch.

From yours truly,

Your Old Crime-Kicking Brother, Dean Yapperspoke.

The Alibi of Siriusus Blackson
Aadhyatm

Footsteps were approaching the border between the forest and the road. I climbed the red, bricked wall and saw that people were looking at me suspiciously. My senses told me that I was being watched. Despite this, I remained calm and watched the people strolling over to the stalls, buying delicious fruits and other things. Sweat was running down my neck, just standing there. I dropped into the shade and watched a kid hiding behind his mum. I noticed he was looking at me.

I felt something rolling down my pocket. I tried to urge it up, yet it was booming down. Goosebumps were rising up my arm, as a black bomb rolled out of my pocket and dropped onto the pavement. *3...2...1...* BLAST! A second later, the street was empty. I ran as fast as my legs could carry me, but I knew I would be reported. I accidentally bumped into an officer.

"Watch where you're going!" he said. "And come with me!"

I tried to hide behind a tree but every time I did so, the officer caught me.

"Make one wrong step," he imposed, "and you'll wish you were never born!" I followed the officer to an unfamiliar station.

Of all the police stations I had been to, I had feared this one the most. The strictest security guards were blocking the door to the station. They had armour made out of Tungsten (the strongest metal known) and electric guns. *I am definitely doomed,* I thought. I made my way through the guards and entered what looked like an office with several prisons and jails. I entered the boss of the force's office.

"Hmm, Siriusus Blackson…Crime: Dropping bombs…"

"It was only one bomb!" I exclaimed.

"One bomb can wipe out a whole street!" yelled the boss, his face turning red. "Right. You're in prison 69. We'll see your back story," said the fat boss. I approached 69, but saw that it was almost the worst prison out of all. *Do I have to go into 69? Can't I be in 96?* I opened the door and sat down on a moth-eaten sofa.

"Backstory," said the guard strictly. He gave a piece of paper to me and I wrote on it. I gave all the blame to Remusus Lupininus (my enemy). He said that he used an invisibility cloak to get the bomb out of my pocket. After five minutes, the guard came to collect the piece of paper."....Blaming it all on an innocent person."

Thirty minutes later, Hagram (my friend) arrived at my prison.

"Ah, Hagram. Why are you here?" I asked. Can I just borrow your invisibility cloak?"

"Sure. I think I know what you're going to do," He pulled out the cloak and gave it to me. With a single smile, he left…

The Alibi of Aaryan

Aaryan

It was a late Summer evening and I was coming back home from Disneyland Paris . I wanted to go there as it was the King's Coronation and I wanted to go see my family. I hadn't seen my family in a long time. It was a very long train ride to get back to Wrangle Snitch. I went on these four underground trains: Piccadilly, Metropolitan, Hammersmith and City and, last but not least, Bakerloo; finally, I was back at the Wrangle Snitch station. It was at least a 10 hour walk to get back home, so, I decided that I should call my friend, Paul, to pick me up. This is because it shortened the journey by 5 hours. Just before I went back home, I stopped to get my daily mail from the tower. It took a long time to get back, especially with the mail pick up. Eventually, we got back home and we decided that we should sleep at my place because it was very late and my friend was just as tired as me. We were both yawning alongside stretching our arms. We had some warm milk and we both closed our eyes almost instantly. In a matter of time, it was the next day and my friend went home. My friend Paul had to get back because otherwise he would arrive back at his house at 6:00am. The only reason he came to pick me up was because his house was close to the station.

Eventually, it did become 10:00 am; I woke up and my friend was not there anymore. I got out of my bed and did the daily routine (brushing my teeth, getting changed, going downstairs and eating breakfast). I did my exercises and then did some of the most exciting stuff in the world! I did some dancing to Kidz Bop and I watched the 1% club. I nearly got all of the questions correct. I was just chilling in my bed and even made some calls for work. I went to my office to do some work; it was a great day, I even earned a new phone and a lot of money. CHACHINGEE!!! I moved both of my sofas on top of my two TVs and then took both of them down again. I went to order a new house near the Wranglesnitch Postal Tower. I thought it would be easier to get my mail instead of driving 50 miles to get there and back (the total being 100 miles).

I contacted the Wranglesnitch tower department and the builders to make sure it was okay. Everybody agreed that it was okay and everybody, including me, signed the contract. In a few months (10 months), it was completed and I moved some of my things to my new house to make it more cosy. As I really like playing football I watched a game of football and Liverpool(my favourite team) went against PSG, then Liverpool won so they managed to get to the final round against Man U; Liverpool won the match by 7 - 0. I put in a book full of football cards and made an entire wall of football cards to show my achievements; I even have the best players ever: Messi, Kevin de bruyne, Mbappe, Neymar, Salahhhhh, etc., (maybe Ronaldo). I went to the Wranglesnitch postal tower to make sure everything was okay and that nothing had been stolen. I went back to my original house to make sure that everything that I had bought was still there and there had not been any break-ins into my house because all my extra football cards would be gone. I spent all of that day adding security cameras specially designed to be invisible if any people walk past the house. I went back to my 2nd house near the mail tower to add in even more invisible security cameras; I wanted both of my houses to be safe and sound.

I had just remembered my parcel that I had accidentally left there and I went rushing to get it; it was an important parcel because it had a weapon that could destroy the whole world. The tower only closed in a few minutes. I managed to get in just before it closed, but there was no mail there? I asked the manager if there had been any recent break ins, but there weren't any.

"Hi, I just wanted to know if there had been any break-ins recently, just asking because all the mail is gone!" I asked the manager - (His name was Jo - weird name, I know).

"I do not think there have been any robberies lately," replied the manager.

I went for one last look. I searched everything, every small corner, but there was no mail left. I left the tower as it had reached closing time. Just before the manager closed the tower, I saw somebody come out with a sack full and he had a name tag that said "Jo Boy". I instantly called up the Wranglesnitch Police Department and then ended up here. But just before he went away, I rapidly put a tracking device on him so I could find him whenever I wanted to, especially if it was an emergency!

The Alibi of Kayden
Abeniyan

One bright sunny day, there lived a young boy named Kayden. He loved playing around and doing cheeky things. He lived in a wonderful home, which was one storey high . He lived near beautiful rivers. He and his father love growing plants. They have been gardening for five years now. Kayden's father sells the plants for money, as they only live in a one storey house which is really small. Kayden loved playing on his *Playstation 5* and always played with his friend, Jacob. He loved his family very much.

One day he went out and he wore red Jordans, a blue coat, a yellow t-shirt as bright as the sun and also a Gucci side bag. He went to get some food at *Sainsbury's*. Suddenly, there was a siren in the next building, which was the bank. He went inside to check what was going on. He inspected the area, only to find there were people laying on the ground and a dead body that had been shot 100 times. He couldn't believe his eyes. He went into the vault and found money. He put it in a safe place, so when they came back they couldn't steal any more.

He was glad that he hid it, as the bank would need to have some money, so those who the money belonged wouldn't be so mad. Everyone thanked him and said he's our hero. Then, out of the blue, the police came and said "Put your hands up boy!" The boy was confused because he didn't do anything. But, on the other hand, they thought he was the person who robbed the bank. *Soon the police will understand,* he thought to himself. Little did Kayden know that he also got arrested because people thought that he stole the letters.

SOON THEY WILL UNDERSTAND!

THE END.

The Alibi of Dora Undiper
Ackschayan

On one normal sunny day in Wranglesnitch, I (Dora Undiper, for short) was roaming around the village like a normal person would. Then I had a brilliant idea of going to the sewers since I had only gone there 102,089,760,067,001.988,876 centuries ago, so I decided I was going again that day. I wanted to see what had been changed in the sewers. I most likely wanted to smell the smell of the nice and clean waters (but actually dirty, I am quite crazy). I never use my common sense plus I do not even have common sense.

I ran to the sewers and then I tripped onto a secret door, which was connected to something. I went in and I saw cubicles, then I saw my friend, Papu Miya Pizza Parlour. He saw me in my undies, so I hid behind a pipe. I smelt poo, and then I heard sirens outside the toilets. It was the sheriffs. I was very scared. I questioned myself why they were outside the toilets. There might have been a robbery or it might have been a BFF.

It felt like I hid here for about one million years but then I sneaked up and realised they were completely gone. Except for one, Joe Babby, the head sheriff. While I was there, I said bye to my BFF. I ran out of fright, but then I saw Joe Babby saying "Hullabaloo! Hullabaloo!". But I did not care and I walked back home like I was an innocent person. So that is what happened.

The Alibi of Adam
Adam

Why are you suspecting me, instead of that kid who steals bread?

At mid-day, I was just watching my TV show called The Dumping Ground. It was a nice, sunny day until my boss called me and told that me that the pizza place where I work was on fire. So, I started up my car and went to the pizza place. Mamma Mia, the boss called the fire brigade! Even though I couldn't work, I was relieved that not everything burnt down. Knowing that everything would be okay, I went home.

It wasn't too long until it got to midnight, so I went to my luxurious, pricy bed and then I went to sleep and dreamed I went to work tomorrow.

The Alibi of Captain Strock
Advik

On a nice, sunny Monday in Wranglesnitch, Captain Strock was stuck in a maze chase trying to find his small, orange, lurid watch. He had searched everywhere for it. It was lost. He had walked so far, however, that instead he found the exit and not his watch. He was tired. He was sad. But he knew he had more important things to get on with. He remembered how he lost his watch. He remembered how his mother and father died. It was like all these bad memories were coming to him. Suddenly, everything was disappearing.

He went to his favourite restaurant, *Pirates Food*, where they served the yummiest pizzas. He devoured his favourite pizza, the *Piratizza*. He tried to clear his mind, when he remembered he was the owner of a shop called PHP, (Pirates Happy Place). It was monumental. He went there and bought a book. It was the most famous book he had. It was called *What If...* by Jason Falloon. It made him feel as happy as someone getting a warm hug, but also as mysterious as the Mona Lisa.

He found out about a robbery after the book and went to the bank to catch the robber and take him to jail. He saw someone wearing all black, who was holding a bag full of money. He went up to him, scolded him and took the money, but then remembered about the taser the police gave him, so he tased the robber and he took him to jail. But little did he know that the robber was the bank owner! So, he took him to jail and asked some questions. The owner wasn't smart enough to speak to him, so he got sent to the dungeons and there was never a robbery in Wranglesnitch.

The Alibi of Aleena
Aleena

In the magnificent, emerald-coloured village of Wranglesnitch, I was going to have a playdate with my best friend, Jemimah, at her house. We had a lot of fun. We played UNO, while watching TV (we were watching *Wednesday*). Then we played board games after we played UNO and watched the other season of *Wednesday*. We loved that season a lot, but we did not finish it. After that lovely season, we were colouring our favourite character in general (mine was Ariana Grande and Jemimah's was Jenna Ortega).

A moment later, I asked Jemimah, " Can I please go to the toilet?"

She replied, "Yeah, sure, I'll lead you to it."

All of a sudden, while I was going to sit on the seat, I saw a lovely, cute, precious bracelet in the toilet. I did not think it was a robbery item (but it really was). I picked it up and then…I accidentally got flushed down the toilet with it. I thought that the bracelet might be magical. It was really revolting and the smell like a garbage dumpster. It was horrible! I landed in a random place with no people, no shops— nothing. I was bewildered.

As soon as I landed, I was yelling with ALL my MIGHT, but no one came to rescue me. Suddenly, a muscular genie came out of nowhere,.I was running and running like a cheetah. As I was rapidly running, he was standing right in front of me. There were two genies; one was in front of me and the other behind me. I was shocked and had no clue what to do.

Afterwards, the Genie exclaimed, "I can help you, so don't be afraid of me and your surroundings. I'm your only friend now!" After he exclaimed that, I was joyous, because I had someone with me. He knew this place, because other people got flushed down here as well, and he was the one who helped them out. While the Genie was talking, I was looking at the view and was thinking of what I could do to get out.

While he was talking, I accidentally disturbed him and I asked. "Can you grant three wishes?"

"Of course, I can! It's my job!" he replied.

I jumped and said, "OH, that's nice!" So then I quickly asked him, "Can I have a bicycle and a shower, because my little legs are killing me and I am soaked!

"YEP, one shower and a bicycle coming right up!" It actually worked. I was happy, but I knew I only had one more wish. So, I used it wisely. I knew what my last wish would be: it was to go back to my playdate. I asked the Genie to grant that and, in one second, I went back to the toilet.

Just when I arrived, I ran back to the living room. Jemimah asked, " What took you so long?"

"Ummm…my things!"

The Alibi of Evelyn Acorn
Aliza

Arguments, bad words, blaming, lying, unreasonable fighting. Is this all you get out of a robbery? Everyone was a victim in this case, but who was really to blame? I mean why would the WPS blame me? What about that suspicious boy who always has his head down?

The sweltering, heated, red orb ascended into the high sky where everyone could spot it. It was an ordinary day in Wranglesnitch—well for me, that is. It all started when I woke up around 5:40AM, thinking, 'What could ever go wrong today? It's a relaxing morning with no-one around!'

I gobbled my breakfast like a menacing monster in hunger. After that, at around 6:30AM, I turned the handle and sprinted out the door, towards the exhausting gym. The heavenly colours of the sunrise began my day as they echoed, "Morning, Evelyn Acorn".

I exercised all day, gaining sweat and my face went as red as a tomato! It was hard work! Finallym after three hours of training, I sped around town toward the lake. I just remembered that I wanted to switch my outfit from black and so I rushed home to change swiftly. Finally, I could head to the lake.

Cracks of sunlight guided along the path and the lush, green grass shimmered with dew drops hanging on. My hair swished around hitting the ground. My red, soft heels crunched the soothingly crunchy leaves. I was wearing a summery, elegant dress that swished like a princess gown. When the vibrant-coloured fish awoke on the surface of the glistening river, I fed them a meal that they always seemed to enjoy. They gobbled it down like always.

Hours passed and I began to starve. My famished tummy rumbled and growled as if it was a bear. I needed my medicine to not become unconscious. Looking in my bag was a colossal mistake. I FORGOT IT! NOOOOOOO! As a result, like a hungry Hawaiian dog, I called a zooming taxi, which swiftly got me home. I took my pill, but it made no difference! I needed to EATTTT!

Expeditiously, me and my friends ordered dinner from Domino's pizza, whilst watching a hauntingly frightening movie! *DING! DONG!* Instantaneously, the pizza arrived. Our mouths couldn't resist the tomato and cheese melting as well as the hot, salty, crunchy fries! Like beastly beasts, we opened the box…

"AHHHHHHHHHHH!" WE SCREAMED IN DISAPPOINTMENT AND FEAR. Peculiarly, a deadly, monstrous, ferocious beast huffed and growled! We screamed and scurried around frantically trying to escape the horror, haunting us. What would we do?

"Curse that Domino's pizza place!"

Then our guardian, Willow, finally turned up with a handy weapon. The killer gun that normally isn't in use! I powered it up with toxic poison and shot it dozens of times, and finally the monster was DEAD!

KNOCK! KNOCK! The police turned up a few minutes later, and began to investigate! Our jaws dropped and we began to question their visit.

"Urm, excuse me, why are you here?" I questioned.

"We are here to tell you that you people are making such a racket that the local residents are complaining!" they replied.

DUN DUN DUHHH! Amy played on her organ, which appeared from thin air.

"CUT IT OUT, AMY" I demanded.

"Well, we were out all day and we just killed a domino pizza monster," Layla recalled.

They then left after hearing our news and we were now going to bed. What a hectic day, however it wasn't over in terms of trouble just yet...

The Alibi of Amirah
Amirah

In the middle of the beach, on a Sunday morning, there lived me and my friends. Ari heard a bell that was meant for us to go home. A few hours passed, then we had our dinner. Mya and Ari went to play in the water. A few hours passed, then we had out dinner. It tasted scrumptious. The clock struck 9PM, and now we had to go to sleep. We lived in an orphanage.

It was 12AM. There was a HUGE FIRE inside the orphanage, and we had to evacuate! I extinguished the whole orphanage. No one had any clue what caused the fire. It was astounding. Who caused this fire? What caused this fire? How did this fire happen? Everyone was discombobulated. We went back to sleep. I couldn't stop thinking about the fire, so I couldn't sleep. I tried to sleep but I couldn't. I felt hungry so I baked some cookies.

By the time the cookies were in the oven, it was morning. The teacher in the orphanage praised me for making cookies and then
By the time the cookies were in the oven, it was morning. The teacher in the orphanage praised me for making cookies because that's the breakfast. OMG! THERE'S A FIRE! WHAT SHALL WE DOOOOO!!! WE LOST THE EXTINGUISHER!!!!!!! WE ARE GONNA DIEEEE!!!!! Sadly, the orphanage teacher

died. Everyone was crying. The orphange teacher was the kindest person in the orphanage. We needed to make the food ourselves. We needed to hire a different orphanage teacher. I felt so sad.

The End.

The Alibi of Amitoz
Amitoz

Yesterday, I was coming back from my long, tiring evening walk. I went into my lab, when suddenly… Crash! I found Star and my brother (Swift the Swindle) in my lab. I wondered what the Star was doing here. I told Florence to keep a close eye on them both, while I searched the lab for clues.

Due to the noise, when I woke up the next day, I went to the cargo ship. I found Star and Swift again! They had captured Florence and put her in a cage. This was literally outrageous! I was almost about to go there, but stopped myself. I wondered why I was about to do that. Looks like I had to go and spy on them… I went a bit closer and saw swift under a mind control spell. I was almost going to freak out, but kept my mouth shut. I heard Star say to Swift to steal something. He replied, "Yes, my Royal Mistress…"

When they left the ship, I sneakily unlocked the cage for Florence. Afterwards, I checked the CCTV cameras, but the systems were down. Luckily I had many hidden cameras, in case there was a crime or a bad thing happening… Firstly, I had to back up the communication system and then I had to upload the tape for the police. I then set up the things she had and left them there so she would say, 'I remember putting those potions away'. Then, I would get the CCTV cameras in slow motion to see if she was there. My plan was coming together and she was to be found guilty…

The Alibi of Jeff The Killer
Ananth

Who was this mean person they spoke of? Even though he was a person who stole the famous Mona Lisa, what they said is they knew that, after that crime, he was a proven innocent person. Although he was still known as an innocent person, ever since then police and crime-catching services were still trying to catch him.

A year later, he was captured, but then lots of people were arguing with the head of the Metropolitan Police. Ever since that happened, the police had no choice but to let him go, but they said, 'If you commit a single crime you're going to suffer until your crucification in our jail!' He knew he felt very guilty, so the post he had taken he left it back at the Postal Tower to show that he was innocent. The place in the postal tower was filled with so many letters that he knew that taking it on the boat again would look very ugly/ idiotic, so he knew never to take anything ever again, because a heavy boat was not going to be sturdy enough to easily escape. Then, once he finished returning the mail, he felt very guilty or guilty about it, so he did not do another dreadful thing ever again! What he did was return all the treasure he had, so that he could be known as an innocent person, because he knew that it was extremely hard to get the treasure and escape from the land! After that, he wanted to know how they knew that he escaped, and the only reason was because there was so much technology, including cameras, which were made by the Metropolitan Police, and that was why they knew all about it.

Just then, he got so furious about what had happened that he became fed up, so he screamed into a pillow. Ever since then, he also knew that when they had invented cameras, they were going to get stronger, and they would also get even more technological which was going to be even more frustrating for Jeff the Killer and he needed to think of a technical plan. This was incredibly stressful and frustrating for him, which proved that he needed to have mechanical skills. Meanwhile, I (the protagonist) was spying on him to see his monstrous plans of what he was doing. Apparently, he was known in 2014 for killing people in private places, where the police weren't allowed, but once they knew this, they were not happy for this. So, the policemen invented CCTV cameras, then removed it in 2017, then it came back again everywhere in 2020, which meant that during the year year gap of 2014 to 2017 some cameras were having technical problems. This meant he was robbing some of the places in the UK. The world was so odd back then, but eventually the world had such a clever idea in 2021. In 2021, they said that every single place which said that CCTV cameras were in operation was not needed, since Jeff the Killer would be tricked.

Unfortunately, this did not work, since no one saw him on the top of the roof, which meant he knew an extraordinary plan to make him go into jail, but he did not realise that once he became desperate to start robbing things, he was going to be caught which was going to be a huge inconvenience for him. In this inconvenience issue for him, this meant he had to be like a secret agent, but he just needed one amazingly simple plan and he just knew that amazingly simple plan. That plan was to hide somewhere and when people were leaving the house, he could steal things. Then he just realised that it was going to be obvious to get caught, so he went for a more convenient plan. The idea for him was to make him tell himself that he would know that when he opens anything, and it knew that he was here he can go at night through a window with his grappling hook, so that he cannot get caught since the cameras will find out that he was inside their house. Was he going to risk it though? How would he know that people were inside the house? What if they were at the cinema? When he questioned all of that to himself, he just realised that he could not risk it. He declined that plan, not knowing what was going to happen, but he just wandered everywhere. One place didn't have any cameras and that was the one-dollar store, but occasionally he found another place that didn't have CCTV cameras, and that was Asda, which was perfect because there were a lot of things there that were going to be ready to be stolen. Then he realised that some people spied on him and they all went to give a warning to Asda about him coming there to steal things. Then he got so furious that he was about to blow up by himself because he did not like his fans because they will do bad deeds to him which was not fair for himself.

Ever since then, he was so fed up that he only knew one place where he could steal cakes, but he knew that it was only 1-dollar cakes, which make you very obese, so people do not even care about buying it, but he had no choice. Once he came to the 1-dollar store, he went inside and he saw no one, so he decided to steal all the cakes. Then, once he stole all the cakes, the baker called the police. Jeff realised he was idiotic and immature when he saw that they upgraded CCTV cameras to be invisible. Then the police attacked him again, but gave him one last chance, so he was proven to be innocent. He knew that he could not ever rob a single place because they were all going to have CCTV cameras, including on all the streets.

The Metropolitan police were going to get into a huge argument in the next month, so the head police will only have another chance to be saved, so he promised never to attack Jeff the Killer ever again, otherwise he would be fired from his job. Then he was going to tell everyone about what had happened and show them the CCTV camera review for all the evidence. He knew that everyone was going to slam into his house and smash him, so he needed to hide in the forest. Ever since then, he realised that if they were also going to search there, he was going to be sent to jail, but he was correct to hide in that palace and he was not going to get into jail. I thought this because I was going to tell the police he was going to go to the Paris, but I was just trying to make it as a flashback, so that they were just fools and they did not have common sense, but they all trusted me. No one could agree with me since I was the protagonist, so I saw everything about what has happened even in the past, which is why I had so many records of what has happened in the past, present, and all his plans. Then I knew what he was going to do in the future. He was going to put all the posts in front of the Postal Tower because he felt very guilty about him.

Ever since that happened, he was always going to bring an X-ray along with him that includes the library so that he can see if there are any CCTV cameras so that he knows if he will be able to get something or not. Sadly, he could not go into the most luxurious building or all the particularly important buildings since they were going to get a huge upgrade so he cannot do anything about that so he cannot do anything. Even if he thinks he can break them they are all in a high place so he cannot break any of them at all otherwise he will get punished. Also, they all had alarmed CCTV cameras, which made it harder to know how to get into the buildings when it was closed because there were guards everywhere. They were even on the top floors, which made it so hard to go and steal luxurious items so that was potentially awkward for him. That frustrating thing made him so furious that he stole half of the post in the postal town again. The others were with people and the houses had alarm security systems, which were easy to tell that someone wanted to steal something from their annoying house. Who even thought that they only had to upgrade all their houses just because of him even though I was the protagonist, and he was completely innocent? Just because of that slight thing that happened, Postal Town called the metropolitan police and then they spent one billion pounds on making several different cities have more security systems.

Ever since then, he was thinking that he should free all the criminals so that they could follow him, and they could steal a lot of things. Just because of the upgrades they also upgraded the police station as well to make it secure so that Jeff the Killer cannot free all the prisoners which was another frustrating thing for him. The problem is he knew that a horde of people was going to try and rampage him just for him to get killed so that he will not be like an idiotic INF IQ person trying to rampage all over the world to try and steal some things in the city. Then he wanted to try doing a trick by saying in his house 'JEFF THE KILLER GONE TO PARIS.' Unfortunately, everyone was a fool and then they all went to Paris, and they realised that he was doing a trick to have some time. They knew he was going to escape and then they realised that the prison was unshielded which meant he was going to open the jail cells and then set all the criminals free. Then once he set all the criminals free. The pressure was on London but about one thousand criminals got arrested and then there were only ten left, so he went to the 1-dollar store to steal some cakes for a nice prank attack. Then once he tried, he realised he might be caught since he was out in the open for pranks but then he realised that all the criminals were gone which meant he was all alone again which was not good for him so he thought about another plan which would help him. Then he heard the news that upgrades of CCTV cameras are going to be upgraded again in every single place, which meant even sneaking in the streets, will show that you were the one who was doing the crime for this.

After this, he thought if they would mortgage the CCTV cameras if he never did a bad deed for one entire year then he asked the metropolitan police, and they said yes. After one year, they mortgaged the CCTV cameras, and he could now sneak in only one robbery and that was the Notre dame. He then thought about stealing the Mona Lisa, so he did but then the police officers said that was your one robbery for your entire year so next year you will not be able to do any more robbery. Then he knew he cannot be going on like this for years and years because there is no point of robbing two robberies next year then three then so on. He asked the police if they could square it instead which meant two then four then eight which would make him rob a lot of stores and the police said I am fine with that. After that comparison with the police, he was so happy that the police had agreed with him. That means next year he will be able to commit robberies so he started thinking about a good crime next year and he thought that crime was… ROBBING the British museum and the London Eye so that he can steal some precious jewellery from those famous landmarks which are all in the UK and have been here for fifty years. After that he was so ready to start stealing the most valuable, gorgeous jewels. Once he did that the police said we'd promised you could do 2 robberies but not in very essential places like the British museum because it is just too famous, and every single jewel was worth a fortune which meant he can't rob the London Eye, but he can rob Westminster Abbey which was another very famous place. Once he was going to rob four more, but the police said that he was soon going to go too far which was going to be a huge problem for him, but he knew something called man invented promises. Ever since then, once he saw a fan of his he would tell what had happened because he wanted to disappoint the new head again and once lots of fans came to him the head was disgraced for what had happened because he had been out of the police community. Then no one knew what to do because every time they put a new head police officer in, he would get fired in about three months and after 2 years they would run out of people who want to become the head police officers because no one is going to be entertained. They only have one more choice and that is to add four more police services in the whole of the UK because they can technically out smart Jeff the killer. Unfortunately, they cannot because they will not know if people want to be in a police group, so they decided to make a trap. That trap was to make a wall, but they realised all the money had been stolen by Jeff the Killer, which was a result of them having not enough money to buy metal. This was so annoying because he was so unhappy about what had happened for them so he tried to cheer them up but people were still unhappy with him so he got so angry about what happened.

Jeff the Killer knew he could never murder a single person. The reason Jeff the Killer knew this was because they had seen him do this and then the police had started chasing him for that reason. In this saturation, they gave him one more chance, so he promised never to murder another person ever again. Unfortunately, the head was getting told off too much because he was giving too many chances to Jeff the killer, or he was just saying he was not innocent. After 2 more years, unfortunately, the head got kicked out because he was giving someone too much so In my opinion I think he should have been kicked out but people might be giving respect to him because since I was the protagonist I was the one who saw everything that had happened and his schemes or plans which would happen in the future. I also created a bar and fifteen more people say that he was innocent not a murderer so in my opinion I think he should be free to go anywhere in the whole wide world. I don't think he should be put into a cage since he was just feeling what it would be like but he knew that he was going to be too wanted so he was going to be chased until he was trapped in the prison, so he knew not to do the crimes he had done ever again in range snitch. People only ran out of crisps because he liked to have the Pringle crisps since they were so scrumptious. They called him the king of Pringle crisps because he ate 10 kg of crisps every single day so that was why he liked to eat crisps so much ever since that had happened no one knew who stole all the Pringle crisps. Ever since then, he looked so fat but then he could not escape any crimes at all so he never ate pringle crisps ever again so that he would not get caught or be so fat. I think he should not be arrested so that he would not get caught at all so he would not be called a scheme, so he did not do any other schemes ever again. This was all due to a war for people who does not support Jeff the Killer and people who do support Jeff the Killer and do think he is innocent and not a murder who is very not annoying because people think that he has robbed a lot of places but according to my calculation he has only robbed 5 stores which shows he is not very wanted at all because he won't be a master crime of evilness because he won't be able feel that robbing stores bad thing he just is furious sometimes or has a you problem because people are making him angry. The only way we can establish this war to an end is by making the fans of Jeff the Killer VS Fans who are not fans of Jeff the killer abolished because this war will soon get too far for everyone, and this war will not be able to stop at all which is going to be an issue. Unfortunately, the police can't make a war because it will go too far and will have to be decided to the government but he will obviously say no since they are going to wreck the whole of UK which is going to create a result of money issue and costs of living which is not going to be fun at all. This is going to be too much so there is no choice but to abolish this war because no one will even be bothered and people haven't been to postal tower for months because they think all of the post is gone but it is actually not because he felt too guilty about what he had done so he put all of the post he had stolen back since there was no point. What was he even going to do with all of the post he was going to do with the post? They are not going to be that important for him and they will not be essential. He doesn't worry about other people's business; he only worries about his own business. Again he knew that he was going to be chased by them police again so did another trick and they did not find him at all and that was when they looked at his house he was going to go to someone else's house and then the police realised that the plan he said might be what he is doing so the police gone and searched everywhere but they unfortunately did not find him at all because he was very cunning and intelligent but this wasn't going to end of the police trying to keep on chase him. Then he was so annoying about to shout in to his pillow.

This is not going to stop until he stops breaking everyone's promise and he does not taunt people about how they are, how rich and poor they are. He was going to need some kind of plan which is going to excellent and he only knew one plan and that was to rob the police station because there was going to be nothing they can do but the problem was he heard that they were going to add four more police stations which were going to be super strong so how was going to rob them. He always knew the old fashion one-way truck and that was to stand behind the police station then sneak into it so that he could start rocking things down. He started to build some metal and then make a giant huge hammer which was going to be big enough to hit the whole police station but he realised that he didn't have a phone to locate where was the police station so he went to the apple company to buy an iPhone 14 Pro Max and then it located him to the first police station and then the police was about to go so he waited and once they had gone he started to go in and then he was destroy everything like the floor is lava so once he had destroyed everything like the floor is lava. Then he went to the next one but it was night-time so the police should have been asleep but it was ok they were only going to sleep for one hour. After that he destroyed all of the other ones he would have got caught but the police left him innocent. In my opinion I think you should leave him innocent because he had done nothing wrong. It was only because you people made him very furious. In my opinion I think that you should make sure that he is innocent because I don't think he did anything wrong. It's just because you are so furious which meant that he had no choice but he had to do it. I didn't do anything; it was only you who had done everything wrong. Either you can prove that he is innocent or he is very innocent.

The Alibi of Anya
Anya

Just as the last drops of sunlight drained out of the sky, I walked into the bakery as usual to get my evening snack and my dinner. RING! The bell rang and the warm aroma of freshly baked bread and cake greeted me. A jolly, plump man appeared from behind the counter. "Hallo, young Ayna, what can I interest you with on this fine day?"

"Hi, Raj," I replied. "Just the usual please."

"Oh, but I have just invented a delicious bread ice cream, only 6.50W$."

I sighed. "Just normal bread, with **NORMAL** soup.''

"Normal soup! Why, when I have a gob, gloop soup," Raj said, presenting something that looked like slime.

I glared at him.

"Ok, ok, you drive a hard bargain. That is 5.99W$, please," Ray said.

I handed him the money and left the shop. However crazy or psycho Raj may be, I loved him and he felt like my uncle or best friend, and my closest family.

As I was walking home, all the streets were dark, which was not unusual, as it was eleven o'clock in the night, and many people were tucked up in bed. At last, I reached my home. It was very similar to every other on the street, but I only recognized it, as it was the only one with a gravel drive-way. Our WG was not there, which was no surprise as both my parents were at the bar on the other side of town. They were probably guzzling gallons of alcohol. It was another night I spent alone, but that was how I liked it, all the peace and quiet, but the main reason was that I was quite shy.

I slumped down on the sofa, and turned on the television to my favourite channel, W-News, then I tucked into my meal. Then the doorbell rang. It was my best friend Salima, who I had invited for a sleepover. She was one of the only people I felt comfortable talking to, as she understood me better than my own parents. Luckily, she had brought her own dinner, as I didn't buy enough for two. She sat down beside me and started eating. Just as the clock had struck twelve, the topic of the channel changed, someone had robbed all the mail! I had a very important job letter that had to be delivered. I stared at the television, hoping they would tell us who had done the crime, but they didn't. I couldn't bear watching any more, so Salima and I went upstairs and started playing W and ladders, to take my mind off what had happened.

So, now you know it wasn't me who did the crime, I have a witness Salima; ask her for further details. I was with her during the time of the crime. Tou could also ask Raj, because I was also with him before the crime.

The Alibi of Ward
Arajan

On a day in our unremarkable town Wranglesnitch, Ward was rushing to get our luggage packed and ready. Ward was living in a cramped, damp house. "What have I done with my life," Ward asked himself. But that was about to change. Finally, Ward could go on holiday. His taxi finally came after what felt like a century.

"It's 30 years since you've gone on holiday," Ward's neighbours said.
Before too long, he was on the plane and relaxing without any of his annoying neighbours disturbing me.

Ward landed in Singapore and the first thing he did was go to their beaches, which had sand like the colour of gold. The sea engulfed the sea creatures like they were its dinner. The seagulls were flying on top of the cafe. The sea was the sink of the whole world. The sand was hiding from the people under the ocean. On the beach, the sand was waiting to be cooled when the tide rose. The shops were selling chocolate (my favourite food), hot dogs, burgers, tacos and much more grub. When Ward bit into the greasy, crunchy tacos, it sounded like he broke a bone.

Ward left Singapore, but he wished he could stay for longer. When he got home, he saw on the news that there had been a robbery. He asked the local police for more information. The police informed him that "someone stole a bunch of letters and that our current suspect was a boy – named Jay."

"I have no idea what to say to the police," Ward announced.

The Wranglesnitch robbery was still a mystery, similar to the time when Ward was in school and all the pencils were broken. It remained a mystery until two months later, when they finally saw the boy on the CCTV camera had the same exact apple as the boy named Jay, which he had claimed he bought from the shop…but he was also accused of stealing the letters along with it!

The Alibi of Arathana
Arathana

Before long, the Star was sitting on a chair, drinking tea. She was acting mischievous, so Florence told me to keep an eye on her. This never happened, so I thought she was up to a robbery. "Hello!" I called quietly.

''What?'' she answered in a rather angry voice. For the past few days she has been acting like this.

She was running outside to get out. We were trying to catch her, but she climbed the trees and went to a house to do a bad robbery. I never thought that she would have done this but she did it. "Ahhh!" someone screamed from the house, as he robbed the money and the tv and also everything in the house. The people were very sad and disappointed as well and I felt so bad for all of them.

I knew it was time to inform the police but i was not really sure so i waited and waited. Then i notice that i should inform so i did. We were on our way and then we got off. "Hello," I told the police. "I have been informed that my friend was robbing again."

"What, *again*?" one officer said.

"Yes, again!"

"She is a very bad person," the officer concluded.

"So, I guess my friend has to go jail. She deserves it."

Hours passed by and he was just there doing nothing but we were now happy so we jumped in joy and went to a different place or country. We were now happy and joyful that we have to know not to do work because without him we can't do the job. He understood his mistake and the police let him go, but once again he robbed the exact same house.

So, the police thought that they have given him to much excuse so they put him in prison without food or water. I lived happily ever after with my other good friend.

The Alibi of Arjun
Arjun

I was at the Shinobi house, training with some Hashira, and I was monitored all day and night, so they made sure nothing happened to me, as demons normally try to attack a very old mansion – which was the case with this mansion. I always slept with my sword, and there is proof I was there before the robbery; you can ask the guards and they will all tell you that I was there. To be extra sure, you can ask the Hashira. I am barely as strong as them, so it would be impossible for me to inject something like poison in their blood. This was all happening five cities away from Wranglesnitch, so I was very far away from the crime scene. I have a yellow sword, yellow jacket and yellow hair. I wear socks and sandals.

Next, I was with Tenten and we were at the entertainment district, so now I was six cities away from Wranglesnitch. I was there for at least the whole day, just fighting Gyutaso and Doki, and then I finally defeated him, which made me worn out. He was an upper rank demon after all.

The Hashira booked me a holiday home at Wranglesnitch, as that was the best option, which was not too far, so we went there. To prove it, you can ask Hashira. When I signed into the hotel, I even had room keys. I don't think I need further questioning, because I was only in Wranglesnitch after the crime scene. During the crime scene I was six cities away and before I was five. By the way, the person who stole it had the exact same yellow jacket that's what the Wranglesnitch council said maybe he could be going to Japan, because that's where I got this yellow jacket. The one that lives beside the Postal Tower has the exact same jacket as me, but he says he would never do anything like that...or would he?

The Alibi of Bob Darwin Das
Ayush

Hello, my name is Bob Darwin Das and I work as a former spy in The Atomic Company. I search for people who are doing unexpected things at different times. Before the robbery took place, I saw the ships departing to Bumble Batch. I felt quite hot, so I went to the ice-cream stall and kicked the wagon, but nobody replied. I tried shouting and looking around the spot to see if there were any clues. Toucans were trailing the path to the port and to the end of the bakery, where the scrumptious smells of the cakes were wafting around my nose. Something was suspicious, a grey shadow was lurking around the opposite side of the bank. I was lost in thoughts, shivers ran down my spine and "danger" flashed in my mind.

I sprinted and ran until I reached the end of the town, where the grey, mysterious shadow was not seen in my corner of my eye any longer. I walked to the building where it was renamed: THE ATOMIC REVOLUTION. The submitted copies were piled up and the copies that were scrapped were stamped with unusual markers. I heard the last hoot of the ship and it went chuffing to Bumble Batch. I drove to the Cherry Tree Hotel, where I met my Boss, who reported the emails and letters had gone! We had to find the suspect and call the Secret Agency to spy on the criminals; it could have been Jason! We took the speed boat to Bumble Batch and knocked on the door to the Bloody Prison. We hurried to Lock Number 45 and there… completely aghast and terrified. I knew what to do, race after Jason. We called the police and they chased after them.

Jason was eating scrumptious cakes. The shopkeepers completely shocked and sprinting for *Help!* Police cars and the Government started to arrive, chasing after Jason, where a lump of cakes went PLOP! Meanwhile, my boss was waiting for the real time to arrive! The special object that can suck anything from a billion miles: The Super Magnetic 3000. The Government caught Jason in the middle of an acrobatic act. Jason was sent to the Deadly Prison where they had metal and sharp claws whenever he tried to get out. The situation was a mystery, where could the parcels have gone? I screeched for my bruised leg, which had been cut by a sharp knife by Jason. I had to go to the hospital, so many ambulances rushed by, collecting people including me. I don't know, maybe Jason must have hid the parcels? Who knows? I wonder if he took our special object?

I woke up in the middle of the night when one of the nurses was curing a heart treatment for Danny Franscio (the biggest actor). I was super hungry, and I desperately needed some food. "FOOD! FOOD!" I called. No one replied. I thumped off the bed and just as I stood up, there came two nurses who were trying to get back to bed. I tried my best to communicate with them using sign language, but those ladies were actually quite happy with my expectations. They brought hot tomato soup and a lemon sponge cake, it was delicious and scrumptious! They asked me medical questions and my health check, which lasted for an hour. After a whole week, the bruises, bumps and major injuries got better. I took my first steps to the road and drove back home just in time for the Christmas feast.

I am truly convinced that I'm on the right track and Jason is on the negative track because he has done everything that has upset the whole of Wranglesntich! Why suspect me? Did you not hear that the police were chasing Jason, not me. Additionally, talk to your teammates, so they would know who stole the parcels and who is most suspicious.

The Alibi of Spotty
Bella

Why suspect me and Spotty? We were just having fun at my house until he asked to see my car. We were peacefully having tea when he asked me to show him my car! Several moments later, we hopped into my fabulous daily transport and went on a ride to the barn, which was in the middle of the farm, and back. I really enjoyed that joyful night ride, as it really calmed me down after a long day of helping poor little animals who were suffering all day.

"WHOA! That was something I will never forget!" I cried. Spotty responded with a huge grin. This was when we heard leaves rustling in bushes from the forest, which was quite unusual. Normally the howling wind is much louder than the leaves waving. A few moments later, I had realised that I had left my room in a horrendous state, so I ran back inside leaving Spotty all alone, with my car keys, on my driveway. The second I came back, MY CAR WAS STOLEN BY SPOTTY! I could not believe he did that to me, as he knew that I got that car on my ninth birthday. Unexpectedly, my car had been spotted by my BFF Izzy, who saw Spotty driving into bins and all sorts of things. He could not have been by the dock, stealing a boat to go to the building, which held all of the letters for everyone in the village, as he was busy roaming around the city IN MY CAR (!).

Even though he was crashing into some things and stole my car, he is innocent as he drove off in the opposite direction of where the crime took place. I ran to my friend's house, hopped into her car and chased after Spotty. We had realised that Spotty was going to his sister's house to give her a gift and was going to come back. As well as this, Spotty told me that he forgot to tell me where he was going. I believed him and also told him that he should have come inside with me and then told him because I would have let him go. Spotty could not have committed the crime that happened as he was either at my house, in front of Izzy's house, at his sister's house or in my car. Wherever he was, someone or something (the cameras in my house or the city) was always watching him.

The Alibi of Bhavya
Bhavya

It was a long day at work in the market. The sun was setting and a beautiful solar eclipse illuminated the sky. I thought to myself, *What could go wrong on such a peaceful day?* Little did I know, *everything.* As per usual, I jumped along the small little pebbles leading to the bakery on Main Street. My stomach groaned. I needed my pizza. Quickly, because of unbearable hunger, I rushed to Raj and asked for the usual. He laughed and questioned, "*Will a century-old one suit you?*" I love Raj as a mad old uncle; not having any parents growing up, Raj is like family to me.

I replied, "Alright, but make it quick, I've got to get home,"
He gave me the pizza and a smile, as I headed back home.

It was about 9PM when I got home. Finally, I could take a break and have a proper dinner, not just an average bite. I switched the telly on and flicked it to W-News, my favourite news channel. At 10, I decided it was time to go to bed, since I would have to work tomorrow. I snuggled up into bed, as the glowing orb in the sky had descended and inky black fog loomed around Wranglesnitch, through every corner of the town. I shut my eyes. But something felt wrong…

Eerie sounds and echoes filled my ears, screaming and panting. I felt like I was obliged to look through the window. All I could make out was a man in a black leather bodysuit. He was heading towards Arthur's fishery and I didn't know what was going on until today.

Suddenly, I remembered that the fishery had stayed open longer than all the other shops. *Maybe they were catching more fish?* This felt wrong and, besides, it was at least 100,000 years since something bad had happened in Wranglesnitch, and I was tired, so I pushed my thoughts to the side and finally slept. Little did I know, something was very wrong…

At the crack of dawn, I awoke to a regular morning, forgetting everything that had happened last night. Before I headed to work at the depot, I went to the mail tower with hope, because I don't usually go – having no family, who would write to me? But, occasionally, I would gain enough courage to go and check. Today is one of those days. I took deep breaths while climbing up those ancient stairs, wondering what would await me.

OH! NO! Someone had stolen all the mail! What was going on? I sat down, trying to wipe my tears. *Why does this always happen to me?* Now I'll never know if I had mail. But, suddenly, I remembered the memories of last night. Gathering up all clues, they fit into each other like a puzzle. Something strange was going on: first Arthur's

Fishery stayed open late, those sounds last night, the man in the suit and now this. They all link. Now that I had solved there was only one thing left to do: tell the police. That's exactly where I am now.

The Alibi of Taha
Eesa

Taha was watching the computer in his brother's room, while his brother was sleeping, and then he saw something incredible on the laptop, so he snuck out of the house and took some equipment with him, so he would be prepared.

So he went out and stopped at a letter box that gave him a great idea: he fantasised about robbing all the letters in Wranglesnitch. But when he looked at what was inside, he realised everything in there was useless. He had no choice but to steal from the bank, so he went to the bank. He had some things to help him blend in with his surroundings. When he got to a hallway, he then thought there were lasers, so he sprayed his acid to see if there were any lasers. Then, he went through the lasers and reached the vault, and opened the door cautiously. There it was…everything he needed! So, he stole it all! He took all the money and gold of Wranglesnitch! And none of it was ever seen again!

The Alibi of Farah
Farah

I was in my house and i had to get ready to go to school. I was feeling happy to teach the "children". It was a normal Monday morning. I was getting mad at some children for being late. I made a rule that students should come on time from now on. One student said, "No, because what if we are ill and we can't come to school?" When Sushi said this, Miss Sophia got so furious and sent Sushi to detention.

I was walking home and I saw the Postal Tower and I saw a person in it. They shouted, "I'm going to steal everything!". Sushi was behind me and I saw her walking home, but the man looked suspicious. I heard some rustling paper and I also heard a zipper open dun dun dun!!!! But then the robber came out, and I caught him and he got sent to jail for stealing the papers. What do you think is going to happen next?

The Alibi of Aleena
Gezena

Who is the criminal? Who stole it? Aleena was not the suspect! You cannot arrest her! She is innocent. Okay wait Aleena will tell you all about it…

It was late afternoon and everyone was starving as well as very sleepy. I was pulling myself towards the top of the narrow, steep road, as I was on a hike. Then I walked towards the Helpful Hotel, which was just in time for me to take a rest. I briskly ran towards the hotel, because I felt as if I was going to die of hunger.

Then I realised that I had come to this hotel before and I had clear proof because I took a photo right in front of the hotel, as its name was "*MALABY HOTEL*". As soon as I entered the hotel, I felt as if I was getting electric shocks, but I was okay and I could definitely manage it. So, I went to my room and ate, because I had ordered pizza for me to eat.

Finally, after a long nap, I woke up and led myself towards the pool. The pool was located right next to the shop. Can you believe it? I know you wouldn't believe it, so I can go there whenever I want. The good thing is that the shop never closes, even at night. It is open everyday, except for the weekends.

As I jumped inside the pool, I saw this guy wearing a striped t-shirt, but I mostly (like 99%)

thought that it was Katrina Criminalana. Since her surname had the word "CRIMINAL" in it, she had to be the criminal. I had stayed friends with her from when we first joined school.

Anyway, moving on… you would have wondered why I didn't call the police right? Let me explain it in more detail. I was going to call the police, but then this guy, who was eating burgers and fries, knocked my phone right into the pool and it broke.

Then I went to the telephone area and then people occupied all of them, so then I waited and waited for hours. But, before I got to ring them, the criminal ran away and I had no evidence, except the shop that had been completely robbed.

After such an exhausting day, I thought I needed to have some fun, so I went to the cinema to watch *Encanto*. It was kind of the best thing to do at the end of the day, basically at night.

The best part is when you get to eat popcorn, especially the sweet and salty version. It was definitely not Aleena since she was nowhere near the robbery at that time. However, I think you should definitely have a talk with Katrina Criminalana.

The Alibi of Hari
Hari

As the sun climbed into the sky, I woke up from my camp and clambered on my horse. Strange things have been happening in my village. First, the horses were attacked. Then the river dried up, and now the last of the crops had mysteriously burned. Everyone was terrified. But I wasn't scared. I always wanted to go on a real quest so I went to the king to bring help to his village but I soon learned that his village is not the only one in danger. There is terrible trouble throughout the kingdom, and hope is nearly lost, that is until I am sent on the greatest quest of all.There was no time for breakfast and I had to go to the peak of the mountain. Up there loomed a great danger. Ferno was in Marvel's spell and was turning the mountains into ashes. This made the poor, hopeless villagers scream as they saw the well on fire. They rushed to their towns like bullets hiding from the terrible beast. As me and the storm climbed up we saw a dark cave filled with fire. Surely there was a mistake! In there was Ferno but before I could go in the cave he had flown into the town. As fast as a flash, I darted into the town of Wranglesnitch with a cloak for disguise.

As I passed the bakeries and factories, The sweet smell wafted through them pulling me towards the shop. The office was full of people hiding and bankers were putting money in the safe. Everyone was terror-stricken. A person selling dragon slime made me inclined towards him. However, I controlled myself and kept my eyes fixed to the beast. This was my first beast I had to fight with no training.

BASH! BOOM! BANG! The dragon crashed into the bakery putting fire on it, while Cremessi kicked it mistaking it for a big ball. This left him unconscious. Meanwhile, I was talking to Criminaldo on how this was affecting the city. Suddenly, the red striped dragon took off leaving a trail of fire on the cricket ground. I mounted on toothless, my old dragon friend. He is a night fury, The city was full of meaning he can disappear in the sky without anyone knowing. I fired 22 plasmablasts so he could be tired. Next I trapped him and me in a dome and used his size as an advantage. Around the dome were paintings of dragons. It was made out of dragon wood: the strongest material. Finally, I plunged my sword into the dragon's heart, making it die. "YAhoo ooooooooooooooooooooooooooooooo!'' I cried as I entered the castle of wrangle snitch.

I had heard that a mysterious dragon had landed on the port and a robbery was committed, while I was fighting. I got into the castle looking for signs. There were massive footprints…

The Alibi of Maximus
Himal

Maximus stopped at the village. It was noisy and busy with people rushing about, selling flowers, spices and food. He really needed the toilet badly, so Maximus rushed to the hotel toilet for a "Number Two" the size of a submarine. He sat there for five hours and his "Number Twos" were so big he went into outer space.

Maximus was starting to go home, but then he remembered he forgot that his belt was left in the toilet. So, then Maximus rushed back, knocking out half of the building. Maximus rushed back to the hotel to get his belt back, but he went for a "Number Two" again and flushed the toilet.

He put his hand inside the toilet to get it, but his hand got stuck! He tried to take his hand out, but he ended up taking out the whole toilet. When he went outside, he heard loads of people screaming and shouting about a letter robbery. What had happened? Well, people came to him to ask what he was doing, and he said he had only been to the toilet.

So Maximus did not do anything and he is innocent. Please do not put him in jail.

The Alibi of Katie
Isabella

Let's go back to the pleasant evening of Sunday at 5:47PM, which was exactly 1 hour before a catastrophic event in the town of Wranglesnitch… Let me explain… It took place at 6:47PM. Here's what happened. The Post Office was closed on Sundays. It stood 3 blocks down from the Local Hair Salon. Since it was closed on Sundays, Important letters were put in a large black bag and loaded into a van, ready to be delivered. The most important letter was from the government, which was being sent to the King about new changes to the small town; however a very strange experience occurred… As the letters were about to be put in the large, black bag, the worker realised the letters weren't in their normal place. In fact, they weren't anywhere! The worker began to panic and immediately informed the manager, who took a look in the lockers and the safe – yet he still couldn't find them. The manager rang the police to take a look.

Two policemen arrived at the Post Office and one searched the town for unusual behaviour from any citizens. After hours of searching, he checked the dock to find a boat had been missing and a couple of letters lay soaked in the lake. The police drove to the Office and told the other Officers. The 3 policemen and manager drove to the dock to investigate further, but found nothing useful. The police officers decided to investigate tomorrow for further evidence.

The next morning, a woman awoke. Her name was Katie. Katie was an ordinary 23-year-old who worked at the Salon. The Police suspected her as the robber. She was told to go downtown to the police station, so that they could take her in for questioning. Once she arrived, the police immediately got to the point…

"So, Katie, if that's even your real name," He started, "I have been informed that there has been a robbery. So, if you just answer these questions that would be great."

Not to be rude, he sounded like the shopkeeper with the £10,000 sword from UP the movie.

"Okay, sure," Katie said.

"You don't sound very confident, MISS!"

"Probably because I JUST WOKE UP!" Katie exclaimed.

"IS THAT BACK-CHAT I'M HEARING?" The police yelled.

"YOU AREN'T MY MOTHER!" Katie screamed.

"WHATEVER!! So… Back to the QuEsTiOnS…" The police officer said calmly. "Where were you at precisely 6:47 PM?"

"I was doing my client's hair. He wanted it bleached, so I did it! His name was Jake Alayason."

"Mhhh…Very nice. We will call you tomorrow to see if we have any UpDaTeS OKAY?"

"Okay. Good Luck!" Katie yelled, leaving and taking her belongings too.

"THAT IS ONLY SOMETHING THAT A LiAr WOULD SAY!" The police officer screamed.

"Just Shut Up!" Katie Yelled.

Katie went back home to get dressed in her hairdressing clothes and went to work to find her best friend, Katherine Bertha, at the salon. She was confused until her friend told her that she was there to get her hair done and she was EXPECTING a DISCOUNT. Katie always thought Bertha was just using her for free haircuts, but Katie stayed friends with her. Bertha asked for one of the MOST EXPENSIVE haircuts on the list, which was for £2000.99, as it was a curly wolf cut, which was bleached with pastel rainbow highlights that were glow in the dark and they would stay for 56 years, unless you went back to the hairdresser to get rid of it for free. It also came with 100 free items anywhere in the world. No matter if it is a plane ticket, mansion (Taxes fully paid for) etcetera, but EVERYONE wanted it! Katie said that she couldn't give that to Bertha for free and she screamed and kicked as if she was a toddler.

"I NEVER EVEN LIKED YOU ANYWAY! THAT IS WHY I FRAMED YOU FOR THAT STUPID ROBBERY THAT I DID!!" She screamed.

"What!?" Katie replied, Shocked.

"Oops… I wasn't meant to say that…"

"HOW DARE YOU! I AM REPORTING YOU TO THE POLICE FOR THEFT AND FOR FRAMING ME FOR IT!" Katie yelled angrily. "GET OUT OF MY SALON!"

The very next morning, Katie went to the police station and, on the way, she got BeAuTuFuL designer nails at Claire's nail salon. She told the police what she had witnessed and showed them the security cameras. Bertha was taken to prison for stealing a boat, important letters and framing other people for it, despite her protests and claims that she hadn't done anything and it was a joke.

"I will find you Katie, trust me!! I WILL MURDER YOU AND YOUR ENTIRE FAMILY!" Bertha screamed.

Katie filed a restraining order against Bertha and got a raise in money at work. She then lived happily ever after.

FOR NOW………………………

The Alibi of Jessica
Jemimah

It was a normal day in Wranglesnitch. The birds were singing. Marketers entered the village bright and happy. The children had their holidays now that it was July. They would wake up early in the morning to play. But Jessica, an unusual girl, would wake up in the morning even earlier than her parents and would do her chores. And she would go to her dance practice, which she was extremely good at. She was educated well, and was certainly very kind and polite. But, one day, a crime was detected in Wrangelsnitch. Before this, Jessica was at a dance studio, practicing. This posh studio was a few metres away from the bank. Jessica was only a little girl, so she knew nothing about this epic crime that would happen next…

After her tiring dance class, Jessica had gone to eat some mouth-watering ice cream, which she bought from the corner shop. She spent an hour there. This happened because she saw her friend and they knew about the spectacular crime. Jessica shivered, wondering who it could be. She tried to forget but it wouldn't get out of her mind. Every day, on her walk to school, she would think about it at break time. She would take out the old newspaper her sweet friends gave her and would read and read and read…

After this mind-boggling crime, Jessica had gone to the shopping mall, which was not too far away from the bank. Now the crime was over, but it was not solved. *Who could it be?* That was the question that everyone was left with?

The Alibi of Jemisha
Jemisha

"Is that all Mr uh…uh," Jerref started.

"J! And yes, that's all," I replied.

I had bought eggs, milk, icing, flour, vanilla flavouring and sugar. I was baking a cake after all; it was my 30th birthday.

"Oh and happy birthday, sir!" yelled Jerref, as I went into one of the isles to see if I needed anything.

Beep! Beep! That was the only sound apart from the chattering.

Screech! When I had left, there was a tower labelled 'Postal Tower'. I thought nothing of it. Therefore, I made my way home to set up the party. When I reached home, I realised my disco ball had arrived so I sat down and assembled it, then I began laying out the dishes on the table as my American sisters and my parents came in. Soon, when everyone had arrived, I wrapped my arms around them, because they lived on Cloud Island. This was my only day off work, since we nurses have to do our job 24/7.

When we began the party, my nephew accidentally broke the disco ball and ripped the banner. So, as a family, we sat down and improved all of the food and decorations for one and a half hours. Everything looked much better; my nan was a great cook and my niece was so creative. My sister's career was to perform as a singer, so she was in charge of the music. When we finally had our food together and our playtime, we rented out a place at the leisure centre and had a blast. My nephew likes destroying things, so they let him into a room to destroy things, and my niece had a tea party with the other girls and me. My family sat down to discuss all of our accomplishments and hilarious flashbacks.

"Oh do you remember that time Chico fell off his chair!" Nan said.

"HA HA HA!" everyone laughed.

At the end of the party, my little sister and my big brother stayed over to help me pack everything up. We gently took apart the disco ball and took down the decorations, and that took fifteen minutes. Then washing up and eating leftovers took another fifteen minutes, and then we gossiped away and ate some snacks until they went home at 12AM. That's when I was off to bed, waiting for another day to come. While I was asleep, I dreamt of that mysterious tower, and the next day I was given a VIP pass to the POSTAL TOWER. I had no idea what it was or where it came from. All I knew was that it wasn't mine, so I delivered it to my neighbour. Of course he was stunned too, so it went on and on and on until…THE KING HAD IT! At least the king didn't pass the note on.

The Alibi of Kareem
Kareem

It was 7PM in the afternoon and Mr. Hawkins (head of the mailman department) was at the bakery, buying things with me to get ready for his picnic of Tuesday, and then he went home and we watched TV

At 11PM, Blake and I were getting into bed, and snuggled up in our covers. At 12:15AM, we were awoken by the sound of feet running on our patio, so we got out of bed and hit our heads. Then, we drew the curtains and looked out of the window, and saw muddy footprints everywhere, but Mr. Hawkins was too tired to go on a chase tonight.

Blake went to bed, but I went outside and followed the muddy footprints. They led me to a shady character, and I hid behind a bush. Then, somehow, the villain shrank to the size of a beetle, wearing the nametag, *AGENT THUNDER*. So, I saw him go to the Postal Tower, and went back home afterwards.

So, when we woke up at 6PM, we alerted you and the police department, as all the letters were missing.

The Alibi of Enola

Kaya

Who is the criminal? Who really did it? It could not have been Enola! She has done nothing that you should arrest her for. Enola is innocent. Let me explain why…

One warm summer morning, the mail had been stolen from all around town. Before the horrific robbery happened, Enola was about to hop onto the toilet, since she had a disease called Poopatitus. She was desperate to go to the loo, but just as eager to have food. She couldn't decide which one to do first so she did them both at the same time. On the toilet , she had a snack or two, but then farted so loudly you could hear it from a mile away! "Silence I wanted, but my wish never came true," shouted the neighbours. Enola gasped, when suddenly…

She smelt smoke coming from outside the bathroom. In a flash, Enola realised someone had set her house on fire. *SIZZLE, SIZZLE!* As quick as a silver bullet, she wiped her bottom and ran to the door. The worst thing happened, something terrible, something horrifying, something I cannot bare to speak about. The jumbo-sized embers were blocking the path for her to escape! "Oh, what ever will I do?" Enola whispered as she panicked, madly. "My cosy house is going to burn down, and I'm going to burn down with it. In the blink of an eye, Enola remembered that there was a tiny window in the living room that she could climb out of to survive. She called the fire department and ran as far away as possible. Finally, the fire-fighters arrived and put out her fire. After they finished, Enola searched for clues that would hopefully lead her to who put her house in flames. Her beloved belongings were all left behind, her house crumbled piece from piece.

Eventually, she gave up and had found nothing, so she asked a professional detective to help with this crime. His name was Joey Bubi. He looked and looked, and, at last, he found who made this atrocious disaster. A microscopic person named George, who should have been sent to the dungeons. It turned out that Enola accidentally flushed him down the toilet that day. OOOOPPPPSSSS! On the up side, Joey Bubi also found out who stole the mail that night. It was George, for he really was a criminal. On the down side, now the only place she had left to go was down in the sewer! It was the best place to go, after all she could poop in the water. "Everything will work out just fine," Enola said, yawning after such a long day. "I just need to pack some food...oh, right, my house turned into ash."

Meanwhile, George was on the run, and somehow ran into prison himself without being captured. He was such a small-brained dummy.

The Alibi of Mr. Nugget
Kayden

Mr. Nugget was gobbling chicken nuggets, while spying on people in town, because the alarm for the chicken nugget store had gone off unexpectedly. So, he waited for someone to come out but no one did... Meanwhile, further down the street, a man caught his attention by acting suspiciously, holding a heavy bag and showing it. The guy was wearing lavish clothes, which were also all Gucci. Then he started to follow him and then the person went to someone's house.

Then he went round the back alleys and climbed through an open window. Mr. Nugget went down the stairs and cautiously watched the man, as he stole $10,000 worth of jewellery! He rapidly ran to the robber and used his chicken nugget gun to shoot chicken nuggets at him. He kept him down for a while and returned the jewels and called the cops.

Suddenly, the robber strangled the police officers holding him and ran for the sake of his life.

Then other cops started chasing him. He picked Mr.
Nugget up and hijacked a police car. He locked Mr.
Nugget in a bag and they raced off. Mr. Nugget took
out a knife to cut the bag open! Mr. Nugget dived into
the front seat and punched the robber in the face and
took him out of the car, and now he was unconscious.
Eventually, the cops came and arrested the robber and
got sentenced to prison for his whole life.

The Alibi of Krisha
Krisha

I was in a town called Bumblesnitch, which is the closest town to Wranglesnitch, where my paper company is. As you can infer, they make papers out of the trees I chop down from the forests. I was far, far away, deep in the pitch black forest at dead of night with my mighty sharp axe, chopping the towering tall trees. It wasn't an easy job but I had to do it in order to earn money. As my van sped towards the paper company, I spotted a soaring building with the label 'Postal Tower'. I had no idea what it was, and I guessed it was some sort of Wranglesnitch thing, so I wasn't bothered at all. Instead, I just went past it and delivered all the wood to my factory.

The Alibi of Evelin
Lakshanaa

Evelin stays in the house and quickly goes to the chocolate factory Evelin thinks that he is not a suspect because he has help with his Doopa-Goompas and there's a point that Evelin is not a suspect because how is there lots of chocolate in the factory. The people that try to look inside the factory could see the Doopa-Goompas working with him.

This will not be Evelin, even if he made an invention. He is obsessed with candy, maybe chocolate. He is probably eating it with some joy. He did not do it because he had a flood in the chocolate lake, after the boy went through the pipe, and also his largest lollipop was broken down.

He would never do that because he even had too much work to do that he ended up snoring in there, as people began to hear him. Every Sunday night, he was too lazy to stand up in the factory. He has little helpers inside the factory and if he was robbing the bank he would be protecting the place for no spies and no people copying or using his ingredients. This will make him sad if he was blamed because they have not even done anything, but you guys will tell it is him.

Also, he never does that because he loves sleeping and he snores all night. People can hear him when he is on his magic bed that is invisible - but only Evelin and all of his Doopa-Goompas see it. This is because they all have tiny magic to make stuff and if that invisible bed brakes then all of the chocolate syrups in there will explode fully and then they will have to clean it all up. And this is how this cannot be Evelin.

The Alibi of Prato Banana
Lishan

Hello, my name is Mr Prato Banana, and I work as an undercover police officer. In the afternoon, I was doing training on the weekend to chase villains and arrest them. I was doing exercise on a Sunday afternoon. I was working out for the two minutes, when suddenly I heard a sound coming towards me. I was running at full speed, no matter what was around me. I went to a place that made the sound.

It was a V.I.P training room in the gym. I knew it was a cry of agony, so I had to go up into the other gym. I was in so angry and wanted to go home, but a police car pulled in to to take me all the way to the big V.I.P gym. I got hungry and wanted to eat my food.

I ran to the bakery to buy donuts to curb my hunger. Then I got back into the car and went on my way. Arriving there, I saw somebody holding their foot, crying. Why was this person holding their foot? There was a hole all of a sudden, and he fell on the ground, dead. Did somebody shoot him? So, now I hope this has convinced you not to arrest me, as you can see as I was not doing anything wrong. I was at the gym. And also a funeral...

The Alibi of Maha
Maha

In a stunning house, I was laying on my bed watching
TV, minding my own business. I started to imagine a
robbery in my favourite jewellery shop, until I had a
sudden thought that it might actually happen! I told
myself to calm down and it would *not* be true.
Seconds later, I went to bed because I was starting to
feel a bit tired.

The next morning, I woke up to beautiful
sunshine, so I knew it was the right time to go to the
shops. I walked under in the shimmering blue skies,
then I arrived at the shop. It was full of food, my
favourite to be exact. Bright colours surrounded the
shop. A strong, delicious scent of breads and sweets
filled up the air with sweetness. Deluxe freshness
brought up an aroma that hit my nose.

I walked in and my ears almost burst! There
were so many people scared for their life, because
they were chattering about how they saw a robber in
the jewellery shop! I started to think that it was my
favourite jewellery shop. So, I came closer to hear

what was going on. I couldn't believe my eyes, it *was* true! I asked them, "What is going on?"

They replied with "There is a robber, and his next destination is here…" (Awkward silence)... AAAAAAAAAAA AAAAAAAAAAAAAAAAAAAAAAAAAAAAAAAA AAAAAAAAAAAAAAAAAAAAAAAAAH!!!!!!!!!!!!! !!!!!!!! I was petrified, I shook in fear, every part of my body was frozen with terror. Everyone was shocked!

Before I knew it, it was night time! The door was locked and everyone was gone! I managed to get home. I got a phone to call the police, but there was no internet! I heard footsteps behind me and I trembled. I ran as fast as i could and….

I managed to get to the police station and they asked me where I was before the robbery, I said "I was in the shops". After I gave the biggest description, hours later they found five suspects. Maria Wobblestone, Astro McKay, Obbla Sien, Selena Dhiri and Yusi Adi. Selena Dhiri looked most like the suspect.

We were put in court and we finally found the suspect, SELENA DHIRI! Everyone was shocked and she was sent to jail for thirty years…

What will happen when she comes out of jail? SELENA THE BAD GIRL.

The Alibi of Timilda
Mais

Far away from cities, in Wranglesnitch in Oak Wood Primary school there was a peaceful, smart girl called Timilda, and her teacher, who was very kind, called Miss Bunny. One day, Timilda was enjoying her lunch with Miss Bunny on a Friday afternoon.

Miss Bulltrunk was walking home during the robbery. I followed her all the way home and I thought I was the suspect—oh wait, never mind, but I saw something unexpected, that was rich. IT WAS MONEY! As she walked, I was as afraid as a chicken. Now I need to call the cops straight away.

After calling the cops, they took forever to come! "Where did she go?" asked the cops in relief. They started to look for Miss Bulltrunk with no direction, like headless chickens. "We have to find her, or the whole city will get robbed!" replied Timilda worriedly.

The Alibi of Marjan
Marjan

At 09:05PM, on an ordinary Sunday evening, I was in my secret base, making a wicked plan to get revenge on Gary Plotter. I was outside Gary Plotter's dorm at 12:14AM and was thinking if it was not a dumb plan. All at once, when the crime took place at 12:15, I was invisible and able to take some corrupt revenge. However, the plan went wrong and it was a dumb plan after all. Moments later, I was hungry, so I decided to eat my favourite delicious, scrumptious, appetising meal, peanuts in the shell, at 12:20AM. At 01:00AM on the dot, I went to my nearby mailbox to pick up my important letter, but, to my surprise, it WASN'T THERE!!! *DUN, DUN, DUN!!!*

The Alibi of Leo
Muhammad H.

The clock hit 7:48pm and he was off. Leo rushed after him. He knew he had to catch him and the Eiffel Tower cake, or else Bob the baker would be out of business. The robber bobbed and weaved even juked Leo, it seemed he really wanted this cake. Finally, Leo swerved round and was able to catch him, "another day, another petty crime" he thought.

Before long he had walked all the way to the vibrant bakers shop and gave back the truly magnificent cake. DING DONG! The clock struck 8:00 "Bedtime," thought Leo. He may be a crime fighting super action hero but he was still 15, meaning he could not drink coffee, so he had to have his rest at a good time. He walked through the dark and lifeless alleys of Wranglesnitch, back to his house. Finally, he went to sleep on his baby blue bed.

RUSTLE! RUSTLE! CRUNCH! CRUNCH Leo sprang up. He could swear he heard someone rustling in the bushes, where leaves were crunching. He looked around. There was a robber that day rustling the bushes, leaves crunching under their foot, but the reason our beloved hero could not see him was simple, the efficient Wranglesnitch detective agency

(I sincerely think they are not efficient at all) led by Jason Falloon (he's the best of the bunch) and Dean Yapperspoke could not see him. If a detective agency could not find him, how could he?

But enough of this! We must get back to the story! Checking from the window, Leo could not see anything, so he started sleeping again peacefully on his bed. NEE NAW!NEE NAW! Leo woke up to the sound of unsettling police sirens. Hegot up to see the detective heads Dean Yapperspoke and Jason Falloon near the mail tower, and they opened the door when….BOOM! The door smashed open anyway and a masked figure with all the mail ran, leaving snakes (vicious vipers) in his path, so they could not follow him. Leo followed the agents into their base just before the gate closed. He heard the two agents being shouted at "Vipers?" shouted the boss agent "This is the worst crime in the history of Wranglesnitch and your saying vipers!"

But as the agents were being scolded, he saw a code saying -- .- .. -. .-. --- --- -- .---- …. .----.

Five minutes later he was in the place the morse code had directed him (main room, 14:17). He soon saw an agent was sneaking away with all the mail! Leo took the opportunity to karate chop him on the back of his head, knocking him out! Minutes after, he was being congratulated for finding the biggest thief in the history of wrangle snitch and he was awarded a gold medal!

The Alibi of Muhammad
Muhammad M.

First, Lionel Messi was lining up for the football match, then lionel Messi scored three goals and Mbappe scored three goals. Then it was a penalty shootout… **4 Argentina: 2 France**. Then Lionel Messi and Argentina won the final football match.

After the football match, Messi was in a hurry to steal lots of money, gold, diamonds and jewels. Then, finally, Lionel Messi reached the bank, but he went inside and opened the gate of all of the money, then took all of it away.

Then the police were next to visit the bank and Messi noticed the police, so he started running. The police eventually caught Lionel Messi. Suddenly, Lionel Messi escaped, running like cheetah at his fastest speed. After losing their suspect, the police stepped into the police car and put the key in the ignition. They zoomed off at their fastest speed, then Lionel Messi was still running on the sidewalk. The police noticed that lionel Messi was running way faster than the car, so the police drove the even faster and grabbed Lionel Messi. They took him to the police station, where he met stronger officers who pulled him into a jail cell.

The Alibi of Giga Jack
Mustafa

It was a cloudy afternoon, Giga Jack was walking back from his late shift at work. He was exhausted because of his hard work. Soon after, a crowd of SSOED (secret society of evil doings) was after Giga Jack, so Giga Jack ran as fast as he could. Eventually, he got away from them and was very tired. They were tall, emotionless, hatted men. They looked like they were working for the SSOED.

After Giga Jack got away from them, Giga Jack went back home once he got away from the hatted men. After that, he went to go and play *Roblox* for 2 hours. Soon, he realised that he had gamed too much and it was 12AM so he went to sleep. At 3AM, he got disturbed by an extremely loud siren from the police. It was so loud that he almost went deaf. It seemed that someone robbed the bank, so Giga Jack ran as fast as he could and it took him 4 hours to catch the criminal, and once he did he went straight back to bed after that. He got disturbed again by the irritating sirens and went back downstairs out of his house to see what was going on.

Apparently, someone stole all of the letters and Giga Jack was the main suspect. He was surrounded by pistols everywhere and got arrested. He looked at the rest of the people who got taken as well; it turns out that Giga Jack had been caught by a secret agent working for the FBI. He got sentenced to jail for life and soon he went up for Death Row for stealing the letters from Wranglesnitch. Soon, he got dismissed and, after the story came on the news, he learned that apparently he had been mistaken for a criminal called Giga Ched, who died from the electric chair. Giga Jack was eventually called a hero everyone wanted to interview him.

The Alibi of Myles
Myles

It seemed a normal Sunday afternoon. The sun was
going down and the wind blew through the maze of
mountains and hills. Me, Star and Wardsquid were
eating patty krabbies at the Krab Krusty. It hit 8PM
and Krab Mr went to the Bucket Chum to play a round
of 'Random Old Card Games'.Then we overheard the
old grill spluttering, I had left it to heat up to cook
some patties, oh that old delicate thing, it ought to be
in a museum by now. Annoyed, I got up and went to
start it again, however, as I entered the kitchen,
something felt wrong. I went up to the grill and turned
the switch. KABOOM! The old contraption blew up
into a fit of ash and scrap.
DUN DUN DUUUUUUUUUUN!
'Oh, not again, yellow squishy contraption!'
Wardsquid called from the other room. Quickly, I ran
to get the old fire extinguisher from in the cupboard.
Just then, person came in, he ordered some fries and
went off. Then, I put on the 'we are closed, go away
unless you are going to give free money' sign and
finished up work. Then, we heard a crash in the
distance, and then screams.
"What's going on?" asked Star.

"Dunno," I replied.

"Oh, must be my tummy again," he replied.

"Look, the Bucket Chum is missing!" said Wardsquid. A minute later, Krabs and Renka came limping into the Crab Krusty, battered and bruised. "Where's Tonplank and person i'm petty?"

Later on, I went to go find those two to make sure they were okay. I took a flashlight and a spoon (as defence) and went off. It was dark out, but I ventured on. Soon I reached the post office, that's when I saw two figures, one small as an ant and one tall as a tickleberry tree.

"Hey Tonplank, random guy, what are you doing?" I called out.

"RUN" said Gonplank, and they ran into the post office vault room. They ran out with the bag of mail (this had my package that I had saved up for years with my one cent paychecks). "AaAaAaAaAaA!" I cried, as I ran as fast as a flash after them. However, they climbed on the Tahiti (some people call it the titanic) and got away. In fact, they even stole a lifeboat when it set sail.

The Alibi of Uncle Bob
Naksh

"Ah", Uncle Bob said after a drink of *Lucozade*. He had been light jogging after sprinting to the park. When he was tired, he got his e-scooter and headed to the green area to play a match of football with his friends. As soon as they did half time, he realised that he forgot to bring his snacks! With all the hunger in his belly, and his mouth watering, he went to sit on a nearby bench. Suddenly, he felt that he was in a deep swimming pool! Eventually, he stood up, but there was water! Everyone choked so much that they all fell down with a THUMP! He ran without his E-Scooter, then remembered he had one. Uncle Bob jumped on his scooter, turned it on and pressed the Alexarater to full speed ahead!

Uncle Bob had always been a bit of an adventurer, but this time he was really pushing the limits. He had decided to travel to Uranus, a planet that had never been explored by humans before. His family and friends thought he was crazy, but Uncle Bob was determined to be the first person to set foot on the icy planet. He spent minutes or even seconds preparing for his journey, studying everything he could about the planet, its climate, and its geography from a library book named "*All about Uranus*". He purchased the latest space equipment from the *Uranium Spacelines* space travel agency. Finally, the day arrived when he would set off on his journey. Uncle Bob boarded his spacecraft and blasted off into the unknown. The journey was long and arduous, filled with moments of intense fear and excitement. As he approached Uranus, he could feel his heart racing with anticipation. Finally, he landed on the planet's icy surface and stepped out of his spacecraft. The landscape was breath-taking, with towering ice cliffs, deep canyons, and frozen lakes.

He was lucky that he would get first class because he was the first to leave the spacecraft. Uncle Bob spent weeks exploring the planet, taking samples and gathering data for passing time, always careful to avoid any potential danger. During his explorations, Uncle Bob encountered all sorts of unique and interesting creatures that had never been seen before. He discovered a species of flying fish that could swim through the icy waters of Uranus, and he even came across a herd of massive, woolly creatures that roamed the planet's frozen tundras. Despite the challenges he faced, Uncle Bob was determined to complete his year at the planet, which has survived to be in space. He spent many long days and nights exploring the planet, always pushing himself to learn more and discover new things. But, eventually, it was time to return to

Earth. Uncle Bob was exhausted from his journey, but he knew he had one more adventure ahead of him. He hopped on the spacecraft and headed to London, a city he had always dreamed of visiting.

In London, Uncle Bob visited all of the famous landmarks, from Big Ben to Buckingham Palace. He even tried fish and chips for the first time! As he explored the city, Uncle Bob realised that his journey to Uranus had taught him something important: no matter how far you travel, there's always something new to discover. There were so many changes. In his childhood he would always look at pictures of London but now everything had changed. When Uncle Bob returned home, he was a changed man. He had seen things that no one else had ever seen, and he had experienced a new way of living.

Eventually, Uncle Bob's adventures caught the attention of a group of filmmakers who wanted to make a documentary about his journey to Uranus. Uncle Bob agreed to participate, and the film became a huge success, inspiring countless others to follow in his footsteps and explore the unknown. Years later, when Uncle Bob was an old man, he looked back on his life with fondness and pride. He had lived a life filled with adventure, and he had never lost his sense of wonder and curiosity. He knew that he had accomplished something truly remarkable by exploring Uranus, and he hoped that others would continue to explore the universe long after he was gone. Uncle Bob's legacy lived on, inspiring future generations to never stop exploring and to always embrace the unknown.

As he grew older, Uncle Bob continued to explore the world around him. He travelled to every continent and experienced all sorts of different cultures and customs. He even went scuba diving in the Great Barrier Reef and climbed Mount Everest. But no matter where his adventures took him, Uncle Bob always remembered his journey to Uranus and the lessons it had taught him. He became a mentor to young adventurers, teaching them how to be safe and responsible while exploring the unknown. He wrote books and gave lectures, sharing his stories and inspiring others to follow in his footsteps. And even as his body grew weak and his mind began to fade, Uncle Bob never lost his sense of wonder and curiosity. In the very end, Uncle Bob passed away peacefully in his sleep, surrounded by his family and friends. But his legacy lived on, inspiring generations of adventurers to explore the unknown and discover the wonders of the world around them.

The Alibi of Cremessi
Param

Before the crime
The clock hit 7:45 PM and Cremessi was looking around at the beauty of the night and all the privileges he had compared to others. After that, Cremessi was practising football to be the GOAT (Greatest Of all Time). He wanted to be better than his arch nemesis (Crimanaldo), his only challenging opponent. He was tied with him, one challenge of showing off their skills will settle the debate whether Crimanaldo or Cremessi was better. He was using a drone to spy on Criminaldo to see what he was practising as he could do one more thing than him and so he could settle the debate once and for all.

During the crime
After an exhausting day, he was ready to have dinner. He was making some pasta on the stove until - BOOM! The stove caught on fire and he was trapped. He quickly tried to get his fire extinguisher, but the fire blocked his way off. He was trapped, he quickly ran and went to the fire station and explained to the firefighters what happened and he alongside a few

firefighters drove at 200mph to save his beloved house.

After the crime
"EXTINGUISHER" one firefighter shouted..
     "Kay!" replied the other firefighter .
Approximately 30 tiring minutes later the job was done the house was safe but it was all ruined after 30 days of planning that indestructable house. After a long day of hard work, I eventually went to bed on my comfy squishy bed.

So this means that Cremessi or Criminaldo did not do the crime.

The Alibi of Creme
Parizaad

Whoosh! Creme Brulee Nel (Creme for short) was walking peacefully down the street to buy ingredients. His long hat flew in the wind, which was not cold at all, but was warm. It was a very quiet, breezy, early morning and the trees too agreed. Lights dimmed out around his destination and he quickened his pace, so that, to his eyes, the lights were as bright as stars. Quickly, he pushed the door open and dived through the doorway. Ten minutes passed and Creme finally emerged from the shop, his face not changed. In his hands he carried two identical bags.

"I hope this is enough," he murmured.

Then, without a single sound, he swiftly continued his walk back to his bakery (home). Suddenly, he heard a trampling of feet and someone stole from him, taking his ingredients. It was Crimi Nality, the great robber. She'd stolen from him a lot, and now Creme was losing his temper. He ran up to her and started to curse at her.

"Don't you dare come in my way again!" he yelled.

Creme trudged to his shop, put the oven on, and started making dough. As he was near the harbour, Creme heard water moving, as it usually did when a boat took off. He looked out and saw the black silhouette of a boat and a figure in it, sailing towards the lighthouse. This unknown person had a pistol in their hand, so, out of fright, he shut his windows and pulled the curtains shut. He continued his work until he heard another splash of water and he peeped out of the windows and saw the same figure in the same boat, except now he had a sack. The sun's light was brighter, so he could see there were words on the sack, which Creme could now read: "IMPORTANT LETTERS". It was stated in large, bold letters.

"Hmm interesting," he thought. "Why would someone do that?"

"Hey, Creme!" shouted a voice. "You have any croissants?"

Creme turned around. It was Crememessi, the most amazing, cool, talented footballer in the whole of Wranglesnitch. Annoyingly, he had an enemy who would compete with him in such a way.

"Just making them Cremmessi,''answered Crème. "By the way, did you see that stranger stealing those important letters from the Postal Tower?"

"'Course, I did!" replied Cremmesi. "That is what I was gonna say! You think we should tell the police?"

"The police aren't going to believe me," groaned Creme, rolling his eyes.

"Well we'll see about that…" Cremmessi replied.

The Alibi of Devil The Killer
Pranil

It was late evening as the sun started to set. People went to their homes and slept peacefully, as the moon started to come. I was having a party with my lovely friends and we ate some scrumptious snacks. The house was very loud with everyone inside the house screaming and shouting across the house. After a while, everyone left my beautiful house lazily and it was still 5PM, so I went outside in the park to play football by myself and had some nice time also watching TV. Unfortunately, the TV switched off for a second. I was thinking about what was wrong with the tv and whether it had a problem. I checked on the wires and nothing was wrong. I checked the brain of the TV and there was a problem with the wires. The fixers came into my house and fixed all of the wires. Then finally the beautiful, lovely TV came back alive and I watched the international final football match, which had already started. The two teams versus each other were Man U vs Liverpool (which is better than Man U mainly). It was a tough match. I saw many good players like Ronaldo, Neymar and so many more.

Afterwards, I ate some snacks and finally it was 8PM, so I went to my friend's house to stay for 2 hours and played some Xbox and Nintendo pro. I then came back home and it was almost 11:00, so I slept in my comfy bed. In the middle of the night, there was an alarm sound as I woke up. I put my safety coat on and went outside to see what it was. While I was going out, there were many, many shadows as I went slowly across the city. I heard a very loud Clang!!! I then went closer and closer to it and a mysterious thing was there, suddenly something held me and grabbed me to the Wranglesnitch tower for me to grab one of the crown jewels. I kept pulling my hand off, but he held it tightly, so then I would grab a jewel and be sent to prison, well the man held and gave it to me. After that, the police came and saw both of us. "What are you doing here?" exclaimed the police officer.

"Well it was the man who gave me a knife and, in brief, I am innocent so I don't want to kill anyone," I yelled.

"So you both are coming with me to the police, get in the van now!" shouted the police officer, as we both went in the van to the police department.
It had a good space as the main chief sat down with us and was talking about who did this massive and destructive robbery and why did this happen throughout the day. "Well, if it wasn't Devil the killer, it should definitely have been some other person," I exclaimed immediately.

"So, it should be you then, thief," said the police officer in a confusing way.

The police officers and I were thinking who this thief was, as then they finally found out who the thief was after that information. The thief went to jail and Devil the Killer survived, but he might come stabbing people again if possible. "Thank you for your lovely help to prove to me that I am innocent," said Devil to me, as he ran off to his lovely, beautiful house all the way up the hill. There was an international cricket match happening in the early morning and I went to watch it. It was really fun as many 6s and 4s were hit and the winning team was Wranglesnitch. There was going to be no robberies forever as we put lasers all around and above the Wranglesnitch tower. We had to go to a place called Bumpro to enjoy the vacation and book a hotel. We booked one of the specialised first class seats in the plane, as it was called Prodeen, which was one of the best planes in Wranglesnitch airport, one of the best airports in the world, since it was full of big planes. We booked the amazing, extraordinary first class to enjoy the seating in the A380 plane. We went to the place, but would a robbery happen here as well or will it not even happen?

The Alibi of Reyan
Reyan

I was underground with my friends and family. First stop was a shop to buy a surprise present. Next, a drive around the city to pick up my parcel from town. I felt peckish, so gobbled down some fish and chips; they were absolutely delicious. I had lots of money, so bought a submarine and took all my friends for an adventure. The sea was amazing, full of mystery and questions. I loved being down here. It was so peaceful and calming.

The fish were rainbow coloured and the seaweed swayed as if to music.

I have been accused of stealing the parcels. I am innocent, i did not steal the parcels.

I work underground as it is the best place. I am very well paid and I get seventy-thousand pounds every week. After work, I went to the tower to get my important mail. Then I went to one of my houses to relax. I am the richest person in the world, and i have a billon pounds.

I would never steal anything! It was not me! It was Voldomer, go for him. He is very cruel and he always swears and says harsh words, so go for him instead. He almost damaged my best house ever made in history. He is ruder than your best friend ever in history.

The Alibi of Dumdum
Rian

Dumdum was walking home from Wranglesnitch from the best place you could think of (it was Disneyland). It was sunrise and the glowing ball of gas rose up high into the sky at 1000 miles per hour as if there was a strong force pushing it. He took the tube and sat on the Eurostar waiting for Wranglesnitch to be the next stop. It took two hours. When he got off the train, his long spiky hair blew in the wind as the train sped off. Then he walked to his home in Wrangle Snitch. When he got there, he rushed in and watched the news. It said that every person in Wranglesnitch had to stay in their house from now. (That's why the village was so quiet).

He tiptoed to the front door and crept out. He headed to Wranglesnitch tower to find out what was happening because there was a big screen and you could literally see around the village. Just then, he went to get his mail, but all of a sudden it wasn't there. He looked all around the tower but it still wasn't there. He was so frustrated that he felt an angry rock grow in his tummy.

The Alibi of Sengoku
Rishikesh

AT 9AM in the morning, Sengoku felt something in his chest, as he saw the sun slowly emerging from the unknown depths of the sky, its luminous incandescent rays of light scintillating. Sengoku made his way out of the house, as he had a stroll. He then started choking in a bakery and coughed up some blood onto the floor.

Then, at exactly 10:30AM, he started strolling through the park and into the enchanted, mystical forest. He saw a ruin with a symbol engraved in it and a gloomy, greenish coat of mist covered him. As he entered the depths of the ruins, he found a creature known as the Nature God. It made the whole forest livelier and greener. He then charged up a beam and Sengoku calmed him down. He told himself it was harmless. He then offered the monster a ride to Ohio and Mr Meow took this offer that he was given. They started their trip to Ohio. The monster had a fiery aspect about it, whereby it made a thermal pulse that burnt everything around it, which scorched everything – even a dragon's bone could turn to ash, if the pulse even touched it (this did happen a millennia ago). He then summoned a blazing rock that flew me all the way to OHIO.

He then finally found the two demons that he had been searching for this entire time – Upper Moon One Renjuro (his twin brother, who, in his human form, was called Misonuto) and the Demon King himself, Muthan Kilingi. He then used dragon breathing, 16th form dragon awakening and almost severed their heads off. He needed to decapitate them somehow.

"Damn you! Kill yourselves in hell! People lost their lives because of you! Why did you even exist and, brother, how could you disrupt the Tinstuni line?" Sengoku cried. Then, after inventing a 17th form, his bright green scrichirin sword illuminated an incandescent green and he finally decapitated the two demons…or did he…?

The Alibi of Flynn Jayson
Rishon

Arguments, shouting, blaming, physical action, unreasonable fighting. Is this all you get out of this theft? Utterly ridiculous, even though everybody was a victim you had to pick him as someone to accuse of being the prime suspect. How would you feel? So, who is to blame? That's for you to find out. . .

It was 6:55AM and I got out of bed thinking about what I shall do today. Even though I hate going outside, I knew could go fishing. Excited, I got my fishing gear on and went outside. The crisp, occasional wind hit my face and the sun beamed down; it sure was an exuberant today. It was good to be back outside again. Strutting down the rugged path, I went towards the lake. I arrived at the lake and got my fishing rod out. After one minute of fishing, I caught a colossal fish – it was a tiger shark! I quickly put it into my waterproof bucket and closed it. But, just as I was about to bring my rod up, something started to tug on it…

Suddenly a vicious, savage Wranglesnitch shark jumped out of the water and went for my hand! Instantaneously, my instincts got the better of me—I hit him with the rod. Obviously angry, it lashed out at me with it's strong jaw. I shouted as it caught my arm, and I starting screaming for help, but suddenly someone else who was fishing had a knife. So I stabbed it in the shark's jaw. Whimpering, it jumped back into the water.

I had been fishing for a while and the turbulent wind started to pick up. The sun, a glowing, sweltering red spheroid, started to come down and I needed to feed my cat, Angel. Walking home, I heard a sizzling noise running towards my house. It got louder and louder. When I looked at my house, it was glowing. Frantically, I ran into my house, where everything was on flames. I screamed, dodging the flames, whilst looking for my kitten. I finally found her hiding in a corner behind my plant pot. Running out of my house, I heard commotion in the village. Many people were crowding around the radio box in one neighbour's living room. Inspecting it myself, I heard that a robbery had been committed in the Postal Tower, and a load of letters had been taken away by someone and until now everyone is the suspect. Flynn Jayson and Momo G are prime suspects, who were spotted fishing near the tower. If they are found guilty, they shall be put in prison. WILL THEY EVER BE SEEN AGAIN…

The Alibi of Jake
Rithvik

Once, there was a man named Jake. One day, he was in his lab and he thought to make a machine for soldiers in war. So, King Tom lV and Queen Mary ll promised to give him a gift for the machine. Then, he started to get to work. He worked days, weeks and months to get the design perfected. It took eight months in total.

Then he finally made it on a Sunday. But then the machine escaped...and it started killing people and animals. It killed King Tom lV and Queen Mary ll! The machine had very fast wheels, it had a very long hand and it was square. The weapon on the hand was very sharp. He did not know what to do, so he made a boat and went to Spain. The killer machine was killing people all around the world. So, the whole world was looking for him.

Then the police came. After two hours, when Jake was hiding in a bush, a policeman found him and handcuffed him. Then the police put him in the police car, and they took him to the police station to put him in jail. There were also lots of other people there to get revenge, because the killer machine killed their family members. One girl eventually broke the machine and put an end to the chaos.

The Alibi of Chef Joey

Seerat

Chef Joey! Me, Wranglesnitch's head cook, was at the doorstep of Miss Bianchi's pasta shop. You may ask why was I, a fine chef, at a small pasta shop? My cafe was on the verge of being closed and I had very few customers. I was here for some inspiration to help me improve. It was now 11:57 and I was heading back home - however I just popped by the cafe. Fortunately, the drive was for 30 min - via the cafe.

Now I was on my journey, at the time of the robbery. I'd reached the cafe at 12:14, locking it up with my steel keys. I was on track of time and everything was going just fine. How could I have possibly been the culprit? To add on, the dock was 1 hour away from where I was, and my house was in a completely different location from the dock! If the robbery took place at 12:15, there would be no chance of me even arriving at the dock at all. I even have a witness, Miss Bianchi - she knows exactly when and where I was. Finally, there were approximately five to ten minutes left of my journey.

Minutes flew by and I was in my tiny cottage sipping my delicious, warm, cosy hot chocolate - about to watch this amazing, new movie. The clock struck 1:00am; I was going to bed, my eyes desperately begging for sleep. In conclusion, there was no way I would be able to even commit the theft at all. I am sure you will find the culprit and catch them in no time!

The Alibi of Kennedy Oaks
Selena

I thrive on challenges and constantly set goals for myself, so I have something to strive towards. Oops, I forgot to introduce myself. My name is Kennedy Oaks.

I am not comfortable with settling, and I am always looking for an opportunity to do better and achieve greatness. In my previous role, I was promoted three times in less than two years. I am a hard-working and driven individual who isn't afraid to face a challenge. I'm passionate about my work and I know how to get the job done. I would describe myself as an open and honest person who doesn't believe in misleading other people and tries to be fair in everything I do.

My family thinks that I'm successful and that was their dream for me. But if I didn't achieve that by the age of eighteen, I would get kicked out of the house and have to find somewhere else to live for the rest of my life. Sadly, I have to resign to my beloved, adoring ancestry (especially my mother and father), because I don't want to get banished from the house. I have to tell my household that…

As a girl named Evelyn Acorn, I was in the dark, mysterious forest. The forest hummed with life all around me. I twirled about, gazing up at the canopy, searching for the birds that sang sweetly. The sun broke through the cracks, lighting up the dirt path ahead of me, decorated with outgrown roots, wildflowers and fallen leaves that crunch beneath my bare feet.

The smell of leaves smelt like damp wood after rainfall. The trees lashed and crashed against each other like drumsticks in the hands of a giant. I was wandering the forest of my dreams, only hearing my feet tread, hearing the cracking twigs and leaves underfoot. A sense of timidness hovers in the air... no clue of what is ahead! Clutching my fists tightly, I kept moving forward. Walking back home, a foreigner compliments my outer garment usually consisting of a one-piece bodice and skirt.

My face started to blush and then me and him started getting along and talking to each other. His name was Jason and I started getting suspicious. Was that the newspaper bandit? Who knows?' I said.

Suddenly, a police officer announced to the whole world about a newspaper thief stealing important newspapers and paperwork to see what everybody was planning for police officers and the government. People were spreading the news about his name, which they thought was Officer Jason Dahmer.

Nobody knew who the culprit was and why they

would take those important newspapers. Why would they do this? Where are they now. Do they have some secret boss or something? Who would have done this???

Sadly, it was time for work and what I do for a living is that…

I started to collect newspapers from my boss (Rob Donna) and deliver them onto people's doorstep, even though I say that I work at McDonalds as a waitress because I don't want people to think that I am a disgrace tossing newspapers on a small, navy bike to peoples' houses.

As I came home from work, my eyes started to drop as I started to yawn. I was extremely tired. Lastly, I went on a phone call with my friend, but started to mumble words, as I was that tired, and stretched my arms out very widely.

After an exhausting day, I watched my favourite programme, which was Dumping Grounds, obviously. I was so committed to the TV that I lost track of time! I forgot about my daily fifty sit ups. After I did them rapidly, I had a treasured salad that I made myself, which was healthy, as it gives all the food group (Fruits, Vegetables, Grains, Protein Foods, and Dairy). Clearly after that, I had to play Roblox and take part in my favourite games, which were Murder Mystery two and Ninja Legends!

Finally, I went on a jog around this huge park that I always go to, as it is my favourite, named Holland Park. I felt as drowsy as a sloth, not even being able to climb on the branch of a tree. Finally, I got back home and relaxed before I went bed. After I went to sleep, something happened and I was extremely furious…

The Alibi of Jay
Shaylan

Once upon a time, in a humble town called Wranglesnitch, I was a boy named Jay. This story starts on an ordinary day. I went down to the market and bought an apple and two pears for my mum and dad. I trotted along the dusty road on my way to my dull hotel. I wanted to have a longer walk, so I went round to the seaside town.

I walked to my hotel but saw something in a back alley: an old man with a black mask. I was suspicious. I carried on back to my hotel, but I wondered why the old man was there. The next morning I went down that alley and found something that I immediately had to tell the police about. It was a secret underground base inside the sewers.

I went down to the police station and told the officers about everything and they went to find the old man. I ran along with them, so I could show them the base. But the weirdest thing happened. It wasn't there anymore. The officers went down, but there was no tracc of the base. The officers left and I went back to my hotel, hoping that I could find the man in the morning. The next morning, I went back and saw the old man again. I didn't let him get away. I used all my might to drag him to the police station and I showed him to the officers.

They took him in for interrogation and I had to go back to the hotel. A few days later, I discovered that the old man was partnered with a master criminal. I was right! *But where was the master criminal?* The old man had to stay with the police, until he gave up the location. But until then I want to stay away from the crime. A few months later, the old man finally gave up the location and me and the police rushed to 12 Donaway Street. There wasn't a house in sight. What we did find were some strange markings on a thick wall. *Was it a secret passage?*

The officers gathered around and when one of the markings were pushed it opened a secret chamber. We went down the ancient stairs and found £10billion, and the robber was eating pizza. "Uh oh!" The robber said. He ran off, but there were policemen everywhere, so he couldn't escape. He went to prison and they took back the £10billion. The police had made everything right and they thanked me for everything.

The Alibi of Cherck
Sherickaa

In the far distance, Wranglesnitch was to be seen. The scintillating, beaming sun shone right above the blue sky full of cauliflower-clouds. From far away, beige houses looked like peach-coloured dots. A dull, grey cave stood next to the narrow, steep hills. Next to the hills, there was a slimy, green ogre with the name of Chreck! People described him as a cheeky, mischievous robber ever since the first crime that was ever committed in Wranglesnitch.

Chreck was known for many crimes, however he tried to prove that he was innocent. Carefully, the ogre (Chreck) took a step out in the blazing, hot heat wave, until his green leg vanished, and amagma, black leg had appeared. then he grabbed his leg inside the cave and grabbed a bunch of ice packs and tons of ice cubes and chilled until night. Just so you know, these special ogres are not allowed to go in sunlight, especially when it is a heatwave. As the sunlight had decreased, an ominous, dark sky appeared. It was the Saturday when the crime was set. Recently, a crime has been spotted, and people are taking the blame on Chreck, as he is the one that is always awake at that time. Although, people never knew Chreck had a twin brother called sneck.

The clock chimed 8:00pm. Chreck's eyes opened one by one until they were wide open. He knew it was dinner, so he grabbed some buttons to convert it into money and went to the bakery. He went to Bob's Bakery where he had Kiplings, cookies, sausage rolls, ETC! He wanted to get some, so he got cookies and then slept. During the time the robbery was committed, Chreck was sleeping while he went hunting for sticks and polished, solid rocks. However, Chreck is proved innocent, as this was when the crime was caused. Until Chreck realised he forgot HIS DESIGNER NAILS AT ARGOS.

During this time, he went to accomplish his mission of achieving his greater fine nails for research, as it had bacteria on it. The clock chimed 12 times. it was midnight and his time began. The luscious, vivid crescent moon slowly began getting darker. Chreck's leg moved along the streets leading to Argos. Once he got there, he saw a silhouette of a shadow but it was moving. Chreck wanted to run but had no energy for that. Luckily, Chreck brought his circular shaped Glasses, until he realised it was his twin brother sneck… The security cameras were on alert, but that was when Sneck made an unbelievable exit and the spotlight laid their eyes on the regular Chreck.He was in trouble…

After the robbery, Chreck had finally researched, and eventually he knew all about designer nails! In conclusion, Chreck is to be proved innocent as his brother, Sneck, who, also known as the BLACK CAT, is truly the one creating the crime.

Thank you for your Time.

Signed by Sherickaa

The Alibi of Shriyaansh
Shriyaansh

One day, it was like any ordinary night and I was eating my dinner: some delectable chicken nuggets and a delicious and nutritious fruit salad. I was watching an IPL cricket match between Rajasthan Royals and Mumbai Indians, and then I remembered - I had to do my homework, because it was due tomorrow. I rushed upstairs and went to my room, and, to my horror, someone had broken my favourite, most vibrant pencil pot. There were some in the market, so it didn't matter as it was 22:00, which was very late – also, considering that tomorrow was a school day. Thankfully, I only had to finish the grammar mistakes.

As I went through the sentences, my nose felt a bit sensitive, since I had just recovered from a cold, so I went outside to make it slightly better, as I walked around the town. I just went around the Postal Tower, when I saw a slim silhouette on top of it. I thought that it was just the mailman putting the mail in the locker, so I just finished and my nose was already feeling better. I could just about make out another slim silhouette. I thought it was a helper of the postal office, but then I realised it must have Crimi Naler and Creme Bruleenel trying to steal the valuable mail.

"Oh come on!" exclaimed Creme Bruleenel

"I'm more slim and quicker," whispered Crimi

I rushed home clutching onto my hat, since there was a strong breeze that day. I didn't stop sprinting as fast as a cheetah, until I could touch the inside walls of my home. As soon as I went to the heated space of my room, I finished my homework and put it in my bag. I wanted to just call the Local Wranglesnitch Police - (but I don't think I was allowed to since I was just 8 years old), so I just turned off the lights and went to sleep. While this all happened, my parents were doing their arduous and exhausting work - Software Development work and cleaning the house, as well as the dishes.

The Alibi of Voldimart
Somayah

After everyone was at home on a Sunday afternoon, Voldimart snuck outside into the woods with his friends. Voldimart and his friends were burning down the woods. They went through the woods to find Jason Falloon's town. The next day, voldimart and his friends started to wreck down all the buildings and houses to find his childhood enemy Jason Faloon.

When he was about to wreck building 147, he turned his back and saw him. He became furious. Voldimart started to charge at him like a raging bull— BAM!!! Voldimart and Jason started a huge fight.

"Why are you fighting me," Jason said.
"I remember it like it was yesterday—yahhhhhhhhrrr", replied Voldimart.

"It all started on my 14th birthday. I invited you to my birthday party, but you weren't happy when I was going to cut the cake. You were so jealous of my gifts that you got the cake and smashed it on my FACE!!! You stormed off that night and never returned. You never showed your face again since that day," Voldimart said.

"But that was years ago. Why are you still mad?" Jason said.

"Because I caaan!" Voldimart said.

The fight carried on and on and on.

Later that night there was a crime scene.

The battle lasted for eight hours and no one died. The crime happened after Jason surrendered.

The Alibi of Jason Serki
Taaniya

Before the crime, a person called Jason Serki was thinking of a plan to steal some bread. It was very smart, but silly and funny. He was six feet tall and he loved food. He loves, loves, loves bread and he's obsessed with it. His plan was to sneak inside the shops and steal some bread (of course)! After, once he had stolen the bread, he stuffed it all in his clothes, so that no one would notice.

I am convincing you officers that I am not part of this crime. All I saw was what happened. I'm sorry sir, b-b-but I followed the criminal the whole time. You see, this is what happened...

Jason got in the shops and started to steal some bread and put it in his clothes. He was still in the shops, trying to escape, but then, suddenly, there was a very loud alarm coming from the shops. Soon, I saw the cops coming to find the criminal (Jason Serki). Jason tried to get out, but the door was locked. When the cops came in, Jason sprinted out from the shops, pushing the cops aside. Then some cops got in their car and tried to catch him. Meanwhile, I saw the rest of the cops starting to investigate.

Jason was running all over town. He went to parks, houses, and more places that were quiet. After a while, the cops got him. He was put in jail. He still had some breadcrumbs in his clothes.

When Jason was a little kid, he was very sad. This was because his parents died in a car crash. As he grew and grew, he lived with his stepmother, and she was very kind. So, then he had a happy life, until he saw a TV show that was about bread. He had never had bread before. So, he started to steal bread and that's how and why he became a bread stealer.

The Alibi of Vaishnavi
Vaishnavi

The Great Wranglesnitch Robbery was such a mysterious and amusing time! You are probably wondering what I'm talking about. Well, you know what, I'll tell you all about it!

It all started when I had freely walked into the supermarket, and I was walking towards the fruits and vegetables aisle. I first saw my suspect at the bakery aisle. He wasn't doing anything normal. He was acting really suspicious and weird. I was peeking at him the whole time, until I fell down because some cloddish kid bumped into me and suddenly he disappeared surreptitiously!

I was in complete shock! My mind was blank and the random guy appeared again! He was getting some croissants from the bakery aisle again. Then the most exciting thing happened! Well, a robbery isn't exciting, but still! Next, the alarm was going off and I didn't know what was happening.

"WHAT IN THE WORLD IS HAPPENING?!?" I shouted. "AM I BEING TERRORISED BY THE PUBLIC?!?"

I then realised that the creepy guy was behind me! I then saw him run away with the croissants and I immediately ran to a staff member, but he was nowhere to be seen! The staff member fainted and collapsed to the ground due to this tragic mystery.

I then decided to dig a bit more into the mystery. I saw him at the road's crossing and I chose to wordlessly follow him around our town to report this anonymous person to the police. He then led me to a rather unusual place. It was a field. It took me an hour walking to the end of the grassy field, which was blocked by a humongous bush of AT LEAST 180m high, and the trees were so high that I couldn't believe it. I then saw my suspect trying to climb up six flights of stairs. *What was this place?*

After a long time of trying to get up, he did it. Yay! Yipee! Yeah, I wasn't impressed. I thought he'd get up in a few seconds. Anyways, it was then my turn. Well, thanks to my parkour skills, I could climb as fast as a…I don't know…a cheetah? Okay, let's puy that aside, well, for now. I then stealthily, without making a noise, tapped on his shoulder, but then this happened…

"AAAAAAAAHHHHHH", he hollered.

"So, what do you think you're doing, Mister?"

"Ummmmm, nothing at all?"

He then walked back to the starting field. I HAD TO follow him, just because I could dig for more information. This person was assuredly one of the eeriest people I had ever met. And, yet again, I had to follow him out. The sky was about to turn pitch black and I had no idea of which way home was. Yep. Whatever you're thinking was correct. I was completely lost. I didn't know what to do, so I had no choice but to awkwardly ask the stranger to guide me back home. But I guess he wasn't willing to, since he looked like he wouldn't help a person like me right now. But anyways, I still asked the anonymous person. So, I went over to him and touched his shoulder, yet again. But I had just touched the air. Who on Earth was this guy? I was walking across the streets when a beggar was begging me for money, but I ignored him. But you will never believe what happened after...

I died.

The Alibi of Vihaan
Vihaan

Jason was living in the sewer while he got an idea! He crept all the way to the bank. Wait a minute! Who is Jason? What is the genius idea? I was just about to say that! You've read my mind!

Now, let's go through a flashback: *Jason was a peasant whose parents were killed. Well, his mother died during childbirth. No one knows what happened to his father – even he doesn't know!*

The plan was to kill the guard and get all the envelopes, but something unexpected happened (read on to find out more).

Jason struck and killed the guard. For some reason, he started wailing (this is the unexpected part) and ran back home (to the sewer).

You won't believe what happened next! He came to a school! Well, not any old school. He came to Newton farm school (a very brilliant school, where anyone can achieve their goal)! He started teaching at Willow class (the best class) and Beech class. Everyone was in suspicion, as he came out of nowhere and our teachers hadn't warned us! Next, I bring the story to an end, as we have not been told where he is currently, but if you do know please inform me.

The Alibi of Michale Jackson
Vishaan

Before long, a figure called Michale Jackson was singing his legendary voice to the crowd as they cheered, wanting him to sing the ultimate song of all songs "Chicago". As he started to sing his ultimate song, he knew that he was only doing this for money, but that's illegal, so a policeman showed up and took him to the post office.

After that, Michale Jackson explained himself and what he was doing so he said the truth. He said, "I was only singing to get money, but i stole the best voice on Earth", so they locked him up. But, as soon as they locked him up, he quickly responded and said "actually, it's my brother – he is the one that you are meant to capture, not me. As they were thinking if it was true or false, they agreed for him to be free and talk to Michale jackson on where his brother's location was.

The Alibi of Viv

Vivarjitha

Hi, I'm Viv!

It was raining and my uncle and me were walking, when we found a poor cat, which we brought home. The cat was very wet and hungry. Before we knew it, the cat was walking in the living room and eating cat food. We named her Coco. That day, I took her to my friend's house, and the market.

When we were going on the slide, Coco ran down the other slide. Suddenly, there was a dog barking. He barked twice, and Coco ran away. I tried to find her after she disappeared. Me and my dad looked for her, and then we found her sitting by the shops in the rain.

We came back home and mum asked, "Where was coco?"

I said as she was sitting by the shops in the rain. Dad said, "Tomorrow we will take Coco to the toy shop."

I said, "Maybe, she's just lonely."

The next day we took Coco to the toyshop. We bought her a squeaky toy and she played with it. Then she was hungry. I was also hungry. We ate our lunch as a family and we were watching TV.

Soon, Mum told my sister to go to her bedroom, and she agreed because she needed to study, so she could get ready for her college. The next day, after school, I asked my sister if we should buy a cage for Coco and she responded with "Why?"

"What if she ran away when you were getting food for her?" I said. She said finally agreed to buy a cage. After we bought the cage, we came home and Coco was eating. Mum and dad were cooking. I put her in the cage and at night Coco slept after one minute. I thought she was still awake, so even I slept.

The Alibi of Crimanaldo
Vivin

One talented football player got out of his luxurious bed and exited his massive mansion to go to his training area with his team. His name was Crimanaldo. He was about to play a match, so he needed to be ready. He did all the exercises he could and he was sweating tirelessly. He looked down at the floor and was flabbergasted seeing a puddle of his own sweat in the training area…The match started at 2 O'Clock and was estimated to finish at 6 o'clock. I started playing brilliantly and the fans were cheering for the team (they were mostly cheering to him).

"GO ON! YOU CAN WIN! YOU ARE PLAYING EXCELLENTLY!" yelled the fans who were cheering on the team. The half had just ended and they were winning **3:0**. I was shocked because I never knew Crimanaldo was playing that much when…

I got a phone call from my mom and she exclaimed, "Hello there is a robbery and people are telling the police that Crimanaldo is the suspect!"

"How?" I responded. "He is right here playing a match." After a long game, he finally finished the match. He tried to exit without people crowding him, but sadly that will not work since he was the best player. This meant everyone wanted his autograph and take photos with him. This took two to three hours to finish.

He went back to his house and, along the way, saw a man with a bag full of letters and saw a police officer trying to get this mysterious man. He did not bother and went to his luxurious expensive car (Bugatti). When this crime was finished, he only heard about it in the news and wondered what happened. I know Crimanaldo is not the suspect as I was spying on him. This means Crimanaldo or Cremessi have not done this crime.

The Epilogue
So, whodunnit, then?

When the police descended upon the crime scene the morning after the robbery, the stolen boat was quickly rediscovered in the middle of the lake, having seemingly managed to partially float its way back towards the Wranglesnitch Postal Tower, unmanned. The newly reinstated local DCI, Detective J.C. Falloon, was the first person to stroll over the lakeside on that summer morning. Before he made his final visit to the docks by the lake, he was sure to question every living soul he could find within the mountainous confines of Wranglesnitch Town Centre, travelling far and wide for any answers he could dissect from its mostly friendly and cooperative citizens.

However, most disconcertingly, there was no sign of his partner, Detective Dean Yapperspoke, anywhere. Yapperspoke was nowhere to be found throughout every each of the town—he wasn't distracted in the bakery, craving over Mrs. Jimjam's hot raspberry jam tarts; nor was he lost upon any of the infinite floors inside the Harrowing-Leigh High Hotel; nor had he found himself at a loss whilst hopelessly stumbling along the beautifully picturesque bank of the Great Eighth Lake, where the hauntingly dead gaze of the Postal Tower's gaping pigeonholes overlooked the secretive, still water below. Yapperspoke's lack of presence at the height of the investigation seemed uncharacteristically aloof and slacking, and thus rather suspicious, in Falloon's humble opinion.

Alone, DCI Falloon began his investigation by unpacking a host of witness accounts at the nearby fishery, as prescribed by his absent colleague. One of the accounts he heard from the head fisherman, Mr. Anderson himself, expressed how his wife had spotted *more than one anonymous figure* hovering around the Postal Tower. There had been a few passing rumours that Crimi Naler and Creme Bruleenel had been sighted oddly hanging around the hour close to midnight, but further statements confirmed the mischievous duo had only been spotted *before* the time that the robbery had occurred.

'The wee barnacles me wife clocked were there the whole time, it seems,' Mr. Anderson emphasised. 'Aye! Not too early, nor too late, to commit the crime, Officer.'

Therefore, the fisherman had made it his business to keep his dockyard open past the hour of curfew that previous Sunday evening, just to keep an open eye on the strange movements detected out on the darkened lake long after sunset. When nothing evolved from his suspicion in the minutes leading up to midnight, he gave up his pursuit of paranoia and finally turned a blind eye to what *must have only been birds lingering on the water late at night*—or so he thought. 'Sorry for the silly mix up, Officer,'

Anderson apologised honestly. 'It appears they weren't a daft flock of gullies after all. I should have been more persistent, and paid greater attention. Then we might not have ended up in this mess.'

'Not at all,' DCI Falloon said. 'You both did the right thing. Thank you for not keeping it quiet, and bringing it to my attention.'

'I wish ye colleague, Yapperspoke, had been as endearing towards me as you've been,' the fisherman admitted. 'Why would I lie, or keep secrets from me good neighbours? This town has been me home for almost seventy years, ye'know. I've got a duty of care to protect it.'

Heading across the lake to the Postal Tower with the fisherman at his side, it took them a mere five minutes to reach the small island, on which the Postal Tower sat alone and resolute. DCI Falloon left the fisherman on his boat and proceeded further up the shore to investigate the island. He came to the foot of the Postal Tower, where the morning mist had only thickened and he could barely see a thing. There, he DCI Falloon was immediately greeted by the three fabled suspects. It was here where the two new arrivals were met at the shore of the lake by a plucky local, who had bravely attempted to take the law into their own hands and executed an impromptu citizen's arrest on the prime suspect. It was none other than his old Wrangolian friend, Leo. Leo was wrestling the suspect in his hands, having managed to tie the culprit's wrists together with one tough strip of parcel tape acting as a restraint. The suspect's face was hidden underneath a brown balaclava.

'You caught someone in the act of committing the robbery?' the lone detective asked his fellow Wrangler, thoroughly surprised.

'I saw him get away with the sack of mail on that little stolen boat. When I saw that he was coming back more, I had to do what I could to protect what remained of the letters,' Leo replied bluntly. 'Clearly, our crook here either had a greedy urge to come back for more, knowing it was an easy enough job to pull off—or, perhaps, I suspected he might have forgotten something.'

'That should explain why the boat was found again, back in the lake, at first light this morning!' a different voice suddenly entered the conversation. They all turned and discovered these words had been spoken by yet another Wrangolian compatriot, Miss Enola. 'In fact, just now, when I went to inspect the stranded boat in the lake and opened the sack of letters—that isn't what I found at all. By the time I got to that sack, the letters weren't there anymore. They were all gone.'

'Disposed of?' the detective summarised. 'Hmmm. Interesting. Who would have made such a risky effort to destroy what they had stolen?'

'Probably somebody who regretted what they had written in one of those letters and went to drastic lengths to ruin any evidence of it reaching the world outside of Wranglesnitch,' Enola suggested.

'Evidence of *what* exactly?' Leo pondered.

'What have you done with the rest of them?' DCI Falloon probed the robber directly. 'The Letters! You took the letters far away from here, disposed of what you had taken, and then came back for more! What for? Why did you need them? What were you trying to hide?'

'The outside world can never know,' the culprit with his hands tied uttered in an almost unintelligible, husky whisper.

'Care to show us who you are? I think you owe that much to our little Inside World at the very least, and the very people you stole from and hurt dearly,' DCI Falloon demanded. 'Remove his mask and reveal his identity.'

Together, Leo and Enola gripped the thief's mask and lifted it off his head, exposing the culprit for who he truly was—DCI Dean Yapperspoke!

The three investigators gasped in unison at the unexpected discovery. The very man who had summoned his former colleague out of retirement and onto the crime scene was, in fact, the guilty culprit.

'I can't believe it!' DCI Falloon cried. 'You ought to have a *very* good explanation for this, Yapperspoke.'

'And there was me believing it had been a foreigner behind the robbery, when, in fact, it had been one of our own all along!' Leo repulsed. 'How despicable!'

'What made it your business to steal and destroy the personal letters belonging to everyone in town?' Enola inquired.

'My business is—*and always has been*—to protect this town, and that hasn't changed!' Yapperspoke vowed. 'The reason why I chose to steal and drown those letters in the lake is a perfect example of that loyalty.'

'Stop stalling! You're only obstructing the truth!' DCI Falloon pressed. 'So far, none of this adds up! You ought to *make it* make sense! And fast!'

'I stole and destroyed the letters after I heard news that my brother had stashed an explosive device inside a letter he sent to me from the outside world. It had found its way to the Postal Tower, and I had no other option than getting rid of all of the letters together. Thankfully, I was successful in drawing the weapon away from the town and safely detonating it further downstream in the river. The reason I disguised the mission as a robbery was to hide it from the public's attention, since I did not want to cause alarm in the town,' DCI Yapperspoke finally explained the reasoning behind his plot. 'The letter I sent summoning you here to the crime scene was an attempt to do the right thing and to turn myself in for my drastic, but necessary, action to defend the town rom what I believed to be a near-fatal failure on my part. I do not regret my controversial decision, but understand that it will have upset my dearest neighbours, who I hold very close to my heart. My duty comes before my honour, and I accept my punishment. Justice has been served.'

Leo, Enola and DCI Falloon were stunned into complete silence. After the three investigators had their moment of reflection, nothing more was said. Dean Yapperspoke obediently held out both of his hands for DCI Falloon to place them handcuffs. Then, he, Leo and Enola escorted the rogue detective down to the shore, where Mr. Anderson was waiting for them in his fishing boat. When they returned to the mainland, Yapperspoke addressed the curious folk of Wranglesnitch, the majority of whom were already awaiting the investigators' return at the dockyard, where he made a formal apology to the people of Wranglesnitch and once again explained why he did what he had done. The Wranglers responded solemnly at first, sincerely disappointed in his somewhat unavoidable choice – a man who they had trusted deeply. But, very soon – and, more wholesomely, in the many days to come – they would warm to his integrity and learn to respect his honesty. And it would begin with retaking his oath in front of the whole village to induct him back into the force on that very same afternoon. Thereafter, the kind souls of Wranglesnitch took the disgraced detective under their wing and slowly rebuilt his reputation as the man whose terrible deed had saved them all from a much worse fate.

Printed in Great Britain
by Amazon